DANCER
A Knight O...

*It looked like being Libby's term. She
had a natural flair for tap and modern
dance, she was almost certain to be in
the pantomime and – what Moth found
hardest of all to bear – she was easily
the best at ballet.*

Moth Graham's ambition to become a
dancer seems further away at the beginning
of a term in which everything goes wrong.
But then Miss Pearson offers Moth a
chance that transforms her life and gives
her an exciting goal to work for.

Anyone who dreams of dancing will
enjoy this authentic picture of the
backstage worlds of pantomime and
professional ballet.

Dancer in the Wings

Jean Richardson

Illustrated by Jane Bottomley

KNIGHT BOOKS
Hodder and Stoughton

Copyright © Jean Richardson 1981
Illustrations copyright © Hodder and
Stoughton Ltd 1981

First published by Knight Books 1981
Second impression 1981

British Library C.I.P.

Richardson, Jean
  Dancer in the Wings.
  I. Title
823'.9'1J

ISBN 0-340-26260-5

Printed and bound in Great Britain for
Hodder and Stoughton Paperbacks, a
division of Hodder and Stoughton Ltd.,
Mill Road, Dunton Green, Sevenoaks,
Kent (Editorial Office: 47 Bedford
Square, London, WC1 3DP) by
Hunt Barnard Printing Ltd.,
Aylesbury, Bucks.

Contents

I

A change of direction

The letter went out to all the parents during the summer holidays, and Moth knew who it was from because on the back of the envelope it had *The Fortune School of Dancing* in green flowing script. She liked to collect the post as soon as it plopped through the door, and she enjoyed getting a letter so much that she sometimes wrote off for a free offer or a catalogue. Her brother Toby liked letters too, because he collected stamps, and they often collided on the doormat as he tried to snatch them first. Toby was eleven, a year younger than Moth, and was always trying to get ahead of her.

The letter was addressed to David Graham Esq, so Moth couldn't open it, and her father, who preferred to tackle a newspaper with his bacon and egg rather than the kind of trouble he anticipated from letters, tantalisingly refused to open it until he had finished breakfast.

'It's probably only a bill,' he said gloomily, and he took refuge behind his paper in spite of all Moth's efforts to rouse him.

'Perhaps she's got the sack,' said Toby provocatively.

'I shan't let you have the stamp from Libby's postcard,' Moth retaliated. 'And it's one you haven't got,' she added, knowing that this would annoy Toby.

'How is Libby?' said her mother, as usual trying to keep the peace as Toby lunged at the card so that Moth had to hold on tight to it while trying to help herself to some marmalade. The jar needed a free hand to steady it. It skidded across the table, knocking over Lyn's mug of milk which raced over the toast and the precious letter. Lyn, at six the baby of the family, let out a howl of protest.

'You really are the most impossible children,' roared Mr Graham, unable to ignore them any longer. 'Every meal in this house is like a battle. I shall be glad to get to the office, where I can at least have some peace and quiet.'

He left the letter on the table, and Mrs Graham mopped and dried it as she mopped and dried everything else after years of practice, and then propped it up on the mantelpiece.

It stayed there all day, while Moth wondered and fretted over the contents. It couldn't really say that they didn't want her back, because she had passed her Cecchetti exam with honours and Miss Lambert had given her quite a good report – 'Moth knows that she will have to work very hard at some aspects of her dancing, but she shows promise and has enthusiasm and a real willingness to learn' – so perhaps it was a nice surprise, such as the offer of a free place. Moth was very aware of how much it cost her parents to send her to a full-time dancing school, and she intended to repay them one day by becoming a great dancer. For her, the future was either full of disasters or hazy with triumph. She didn't see that life tends to be a more settled affair with less extreme ups and downs, and that what usually happens is something unexpected.

8

And so it proved with the letter, when her father was finally persuaded to open it that evening. He read it to himself first, while Moth watched anxiously, and then he read it aloud.

Dear Mr Graham,
I am writing to you to let you know about some exciting changes that will be happening next term.

As you are probably aware, small schools like ours have constant financial problems in these inflationary times, when even something as simple as the heating costs can threaten to overwhelm our entire budget. We are, however, determined to keep up our high standards.

Many parents are naturally concerned about the future opportunities open to our students, and I know that some of you are worried by the strong competition that exists in the world of ballet. Some of our pupils already realise that they are not going to make the grade as dancers and would welcome the chance to broaden their training to equip them for the wider world of the theatre. In the past, this has not been possible at the Fortune, but we are now able to join forces with another school near-by that specialises in general training for the stage.

This does not mean that there will be any changes to the ballet classes, but we shall now be able to offer professional tuition in speech and drama as well as a much wider range of dancing. It also means that any pupils advised not to concentrate solely on ballet, will be able to transfer to other courses without having to change schools.

I enclose a list of the optional extras that will now be available, and I shall be glad to discuss them with you.

'And there's a long list of extras such as modern dance, tap, music, voice training, fencing, make-up, etc., in case you're interested,' he added, offering the letter to Moth.

'I'm not,' she said firmly.

'I think it sounds a good idea,' said her mother. 'I'm sure these little schools must be having a very worrying time, and it makes sense for them to band together like this.'

Moth looked unconvinced. 'I liked the Fortune the way it was,' she said. 'It was all about dancing, *proper* dancing. Now we shall have more people like that awful Selsey James, who didn't know the first thing about ballet and spent all her time showing off.'

'That was the child who did that clever tap dance, wasn't it? I thought she was rather precocious, but then if you want to get on in the theatre, you'll have to learn to cope with people like that. After all, acting is about showing off, isn't it?'

'But I don't want to be an actress,' said Moth. 'I want to be a dancer, and that's quite different. You never understand,' she added, suddenly furious, 'because it just seems like a game to you.'

'Don't talk to your mother like that,' said her father sharply. 'She understands to the extent of doing a job to help pay for your dancing.'

Moth was silent, and then said a quiet 'Sorry'. She really was sorry, but dancing had become the most important thing in her life, and increasingly it seemed to cut her off from her parents. She couldn't help feeling intense about ballet, and yet she couldn't share this intensity with them. She herself didn't yet know much about the world of ballet, but to them it meant only the one or two performances they had taken her to, and she suspected that her father hadn't enjoyed those all that much! Certainly they had no idea how much the prospect of becoming a dancer lit up Moth's future. They were ready to wait and see what life offered and then make the best of it, whereas she longed to be swept away, to be totally dedicated, to work impossible hours, if it would bring her the kind of involvement that was so different from her parents' own lives.

In the week before the new term began Moth often found herself thinking about the possible changes that might lie ahead. Last year she had been faced with a new school and with leaving home to live with an unknown relation. Now, although she had become fond of her great-aunt and looked forward to going back to a proper room of her own where there was space to arrange all her possessions, there was something else to worry about.

She wondered how her cousin Libby would react. Libby had gone back to Australia for the summer, and her occasional postcards were all about the sun and swimming. Her attitude to dancing, and to everything else, was far more happy-go-lucky, but she was just as determined as Moth and would surely share her concern at seeing the school invaded by a pack of stage-struck brats who were probably hopeless at ballet.

Moth and her father drove up to London past fields burnished by an autumn sun. The summer itself had been cool and wet, so that the children had been forced to stay indoors, but now that the holidays were over, it was irritatingly warm. Moth almost wished it were raining; she was impatient to get on with a term that was traditionally cold and dark, so that one was glad to hurry home.

Act one, scene one, she thought, as she tumbled out of the car, ran to the side door that led up to her great-aunt's top flat, and pressed the buzzer. The house-phone was one of her great-aunt's rare concessions to the modern world, and Moth expected to hear her firm voice asking, 'Who's there?' But no one replied, and there was no sound of answering footsteps. Her father, who had been getting her cases out of the boot, came up the path and she rang again, this time sensing that the buzzer was disturbing an empty flat.

He looked surprised. 'That's odd. Marion knew we were coming this afternoon. Your mother rang up and told her.'

Moth sat down on the broad stone step while her father paced round the front garden, looking critically at some wayward tasselled fuchias that had more blooms than his own neat, well-cared-for ones. Finally, he said, 'I don't like leaving you out on the pavement, but I really ought to be getting back. I was hoping to get out of London before all those dedicated commuters. You know how I hate that head-to-tail driving.'

'You don't have to stay,' said Moth. 'I expect Great-Aunt Marion's just popped round to the shops or gone to change her library book. You can leave me here. I'll be quite safe.'

Last year she had clung to him, but now she was happy to see him go. Not because she didn't love him just as much, but because she wanted to get on with her own life and assert her independence.

Her father looked at his watch. 'You're sure you won't mind if I get along? Tell Marion I'm very sorry to have missed her and explain the situation. I expect she'll turn up as soon as I've gone.'

He looked a little uneasy at deserting her, so Moth gave him a reassuring hug. 'I'll ring up this evening so you'll know I'm not still on the doorstep,' she promised, and waved him away. As the car slid round the corner, the street, drowsy with sunshine, went back to sleep.

Moth explored the feeling of freedom. I'm all by myself in London, she thought. I could go anywhere, spend my pocket money on anything. She dawdled along the path, watched closely by an inquisitive cat. She made a move to stroke it, but it leapt out of reach and went on watching her from the top of the wall. Moth picked up the green casing of a chestnut that had probably been knocked off the tree by some impatient small boy. It had split in falling, and she eased it open and prised out the glossy nut. She had once collected conkers, until she had become saddened by the way they soon lost their sheen and shrivelled up. I wonder if Lyn knows how to make them into chairs for her doll's house, she thought, remembering how she had given hers pin legs and woven the backs with embroidery silks. The nut glowed in her hand as she traced the map of its growth while speculating about her great-aunt.

Supposing she had been taken ill and rushed off to hospital. Or tripped over a kerb and broken her leg. Old people often died suddenly. Supposing the flat wasn't empty, and in bed or on the floor lay . . . Moth was in the middle of deciding that by six o'clock she would call for the police when her forebodings were shattered by Libby's unmistakable voice.

'Look who's here,' she called to a figure who, miraculously, wasn't dead after all but wrestling with the gate, which was obstinately refusing to stay shut.

'My dear child,' said Great-Aunt Marion, hastening round the side of the house, 'where's your father?'

'Daddy had to get back,' Moth explained, 'to avoid being stuck in a jam.'

'I knew we shouldn't have gone shopping, but Libby was so insistent, and I thought we'd be back in time. I'd prepared a special tea for your father,' she added, as

13

they went upstairs. 'What must he have thought?'

'All the more for us,' said Libby callously. She was as brown as a sailor and the sun had streaked her hair with fairer highlights. 'I'm going to try on my new shoes,' and she darted away.

'I suppose we might as well have tea,' said Great-Aunt Marion, who was fond of her nephew and had made scones and a rich cake dark with fruit to please him. 'Take these into the other room, will you.'

Moth carried the things that wouldn't fit on to the trolley into the living room. Everything was grander than at home, from the huge old-fashioned settee with its cane arms and massive velvet cushions to the carved sideboard crowded with ornaments that her great-aunt could safely display because there was no Toby to start landing on the moon and no Lyn to spill paintwater on the polished surface. It was a home that reflected the order and comfort of old age, not a place for growing, exploring, stretching, and breaking.

Moth could see specks of dust in the slanting spotlights of sun. The room smelled of apples – there was a bowl of them on the table – and of rose petals blurred with spices.

She separated the nest of small tables and arranged them near the settee. Her great-aunt wheeled in the trolley of tea-things and then said, 'Perhaps you'd rather have orange juice. It'll take me a little time to get back to your ways.'

'No, tea for me, please.' Moth didn't much like her great-aunt's brand of tea, which was very pale and had leaves the size of stalks in it, but she didn't want to be a child with childish tastes.

'I think you've grown,' said her great-aunt as she poured out the tea. The cups had a faded line of gold round the rim; inside a pattern of full-blown roses just

14

showed above the fragrant tea. 'And your hair's longer too, though you certainly haven't put on any weight. I can't think where all those crisps and ice-creams go.'

'Mummy wanted me to have my hair cut,' said Moth, turning her head so that her great-aunt could see that her hair now reached the middle of her back. 'She thinks it's untidy and it takes ages to dry, but I like it extra long. It looks right for a dancer, and it makes up for its being so very straight and such an ordinary brown.'

'That runs in our family; I don't know where Libby's fair waves come from. My hair used to be just like yours before it went white.'

As usual, Great-Aunt Marion's hair was pinned up in a neat French pleat. It suits her, thought Moth, surprised to see that her great-aunt looked less severe than she remembered. She hadn't realised that old people changed, but although her great-aunt was as elegant and upright as ever, she had altered, though in a less obvious way than Moth. She recalled her mother saying that people tended to shrink as they got older, whereas at Moth's age – which was twelve – they went on shooting up. Perhaps that was it.

Moth was trying to fit everything on to her little table and manoeuvre the jam without spilling it, when there was a clatter on the stairs from the attic and Libby pranced into the room.

'Listen,' she said, shuffling her feet on the parquet floor.

'Not on my floor!' cried Great-Aunt Marion in anguish, while Moth stared in horror at Libby's shoes.

'Aren't they great!' Libby threw herself on to the settee, grabbed a scone and held up her feet for Moth's approval.

Moth looked at the shiny laced shoes with their steel

16

rimmed heels and tipped toes. 'They're tap shoes,' she said in disgust.

'Sure. Aren't you going to get some?' Libby's enthusiasm was muffled by the scone. 'Didn't you get a letter about the changes at the school? I've persuaded Dad to let me do tap and modern dance. He's much more keen on the school now there are so many more opportunities.'

Moth's heart sank. 'I'm just doing ballet,' she said coldly, 'because it's all I've ever wanted to do. And I thought you felt the same.'

Libby took no notice of the implied accusation. 'I do. I love ballet, but I want to try everything else as well. And I want to take part in a proper show and get real stage experience. You can't do that with ballet, because there aren't any ballets for children.'

There was no answer, because Moth knew she was right. She remembered reading that there were no parts for children in most ballets, and those there were, were usually danced by professionals.

Libby attacked the fruit cake but Moth didn't want any. So this was what the new term was going to be like. She saw that everyone would feel like Libby and want to seize the chance of appearing on the stage. It was what she wanted too, but not as some kind of chorus girl or in a pantomime. Surely, she thought miserably, as Libby prattled confidently on about the future, this wasn't the kind of start that might one day lead to the stage of Covent Garden.

A quarrel

'I want to start,' said Miss Pearson, looking round the attentive circle of girls in blue leotards and pink tights sitting on the floor at the end of class, 'with an awful warning. I know you've all been longing for the moment when you can start wearing pointe shoes, but if you start dancing on your pointes before your feet are strong enough, you'll not only ruin any chance you may have of becoming a dancer, but you could also cripple yourself for life.'

Moth, who had bought her first pair of pointe shoes during the holidays, wondered whether trying them on in front of the mirror while balancing with the help of a chair could have done any harm. Surely not.

'I know,' continued Miss Pearson, 'that granny and auntie and all your friends don't think you're a real dancer unless you can stand on your toes, but impressing them isn't worth the risk. As far as this class is concerned, we shall be doing just a few minutes' pointe work at the end of class for quite a time, and I may have to stop some of you if it becomes clear that your feet aren't ready yet. Now, any questions?'

19

'Is there anything you can do if your feet aren't right?' asked Jane Montagu, who had inherited her ballet ambitions from her parents. They were ardent balletomanes who were always taking Jane to Covent Garden, and they were willing to spend any amount on helping their daughter to become a dancer.

'A certain amount, yes, if you're sensible,' said Miss Pearson, 'but of course you can't change the basic shape of your foot. Some feet seem to have been designed for the job, while others need a lot of patient exercise and even then may find the strain too much. But cheer up. We had a good look at your feet before you were admitted, so the chances are that you'll be all right. And I expect your feet were examined too,' she added, looking at the new recruits from the stage school. None of them seemed to have any doubts, not even the skinny girl who giggled pathetically every time she went wrong. They're so horribly confident, thought Moth.

'So, we'll begin by hoping that you've all got strong feet, and the first thing you have to learn is how to look after your shoes.'

Moth picked up her shoes with the feeling that at last she was about to take off. She would come to resent the amount of time that had to be spent darning pointe shoes, but at this moment it was a welcome chore, a step nearer to becoming a proper dancer.

'If you examine the toes of your shoes,' Miss Pearson went on, 'you'll see that the stiff point has been squared off to make a flat end. This is what you balance on, and to make the satin on this part less slippery and to help it to last longer, most dancers slit the satin and then darn the toe. And that's what you're all going to do.'

'Do we have to?' asked Jane, who hated any kind of sewing. 'Can't we just cut the satin off like professional dancers do? My mother knows someone in the Royal

Ballet, and she never darns her shoes.'

'No doubt she doesn't have the time,' said Miss Pearson tartly, 'but at the moment you do. So no matter how much money your parents are prepared to spend on your shoes – and I doubt if they will really want to keep buying them – you'll have to darn your shoes like everyone else. Unless you can persuade your mother to do it for you.'

The class laughed, but Moth doubted whether they really saw the joke. She remembered seeing the elegant Mrs Montagu at the summer show and had noticed her beautifully manicured hands with their long tapering nails. They would never do for darning.

'And before you start hacking your shoes about,' went on Miss Pearson remorselessly, 'I should explain that there is a special way of darning them which Mrs George will show you in your next sewing lesson, and I shall then examine them to make sure that you've done the job properly. *Properly,*' she emphasised, looking at Jane. 'And while I'm on the subject of shoes, I notice that one or two of you are getting very careless at tying them. I shouldn't have to scold the second year about this, but I don't want to see any ribbon-ends showing, so see that you tuck them in. As most of you already know, I expect you to pay the same attention to your appearance as you do to your dancing. Right, off you go.'

The class gathered up their things, curtsied to Miss Pearson, and trooped away. Most of them, including Libby, had a tap class next, and Moth found herself the only person in the cloakroom. As she took off her practice things and rummaged in her locker for her shirt and pullover and skirt, she remembered that Ruth hadn't been at class. She was certainly not away – Moth had sat next to her for geography – but Ruth had only turned up at the last minute and then dashed off without

21

a word as soon as the bell went. They hadn't had a chance to talk the day before either. When they were together, it was always as part of a group, and although Moth had looked forward to their walking home together, she had not been able to find Ruth after school and so had tagged along with Libby and Tom, who were swapping boasts about how far they could swim.

Moth had come to think of Ruth as her best friend, and it meant a lot to her to have someone with whom she could share her plans for the future. Ruth, too, had set her heart on becoming a dancer, and she came from a home that encouraged this as a natural, worthwhile ambition. Unlike Moth's parents, who had nothing against music and books but never went to a concert or read anything more demanding than a thriller, the Fishers had a house spilling over with books and records.

When she had gone to tea there, Moth had been impressed by the shelves of books, some of them scattered round in a casual way as though the reader had only just been interrupted. And after tea they had gone into the garden to leave the drawing room free for Ruth's brother, who wanted to be a concert pianist, to practise. Moth didn't like him much – he had an offhand manner that suggested he found her and Ruth tiresome little girls – but she was surprised by the magical sound that came from the piano. It was so unlike the instruments at school, that churned out the tunes and rhythms of a class. Daniel made the notes trickle and shiver and fly through the air like spray. She wanted to stay by the window and listen, but Ruth, who was used to a house full of music and a brother who practised for hours every day, dragged her away to try the hammock she had rigged up at the bottom of the garden.

Everything in the house offered an intriguing glimpse of a world she hardly knew existed. Moth would like to have stayed there for a while to get to know the drawings, paintings, prints, that hung in every room, and absorb the books. It wasn't a question of reading them all, but the feeling that if she were to live among them they would rub off on her, just as by hearing Daniel practise every day she would be breathing in music.

I hope she'll ask me again soon, she thought, as she pushed her things into her locker. Someone else had come into the cloakroom and, as though in answer to her thoughts, she saw it was Ruth.

'Where have you been?' she called out, slamming the door of her locker and darting towards Ruth. 'Why didn't you come to class? We're going to wear our pointe shoes at last, and you missed Miss P.'s awful warning about how we're all going to be crippled with blisters and arthritis.'

Ruth made no reply. She was wearing her leotard and tights as though she had got ready for class, and she held her hands behind her back as though she was hiding something. Her round face was as red as a poppy, and Moth's first thought was that she must be ill.

'What's the matter?' she said. 'Don't you feel well? Would you like me to tell someone or come home with you?'

Ruth looked uneasy and embarrassed, and she looked down instead of at Moth. 'I'm all right,' she said in a low voice, and then added in a rush, 'If you really want to know, I didn't come to class because I've given up ballet.'

Moth stared at her in disbelief. 'Given up ballet,' she repeated. 'But you can't have done. You care about it as much as I do, and we agreed it's the only thing in life worth doing. We planned to audition for the Upper School of the R.B., don't you remember?'

'Well, I've changed my mind. I've realised that I'm

23

not good enough to become a professional dancer, and it seems silly to go on working at something when you know it's all for nothing.'

Ruth backed away from Moth, as though to escape from her accusing stare. She still had her hands behind her back, and there was something about the unnatural position of her arms that roused Moth's suspicion. She jumped forward and seized Ruth's arm fiercely. Taken off guard, Ruth dropped what she was holding on to the floor. It was a steel-tipped shoe.

'You're not learning to tap,' Moth said indignantly.

'It's none of your business.'

'But last year you said you hated it as much as I do. We agreed that it's not for real dancers but for chorus-girls like that dreadful little show-off Selsey. You can't really be giving up ballet and taking up tap instead?'

Moth's tone was bitter and scornful, but that wasn't the way she felt inside. She had so looked forward to sharing class with Ruth, and had counted on her support in upholding what Moth felt, in an illogical, instinctive way, were the standards of *real* dancing. She didn't like tap, she'd never liked tap, and even if she was wrong – and she wasn't quite so sure now that she might not be wrong – she wanted an ally. She wasn't really surprised that Libby wanted to do tap – Libby had a go at everything and didn't need a sense of dedication – but she had counted on Ruth understanding how she felt, and feeling the same way too.

But Ruth couldn't be expected to see that. She had known that Moth would mind, because she herself minded so much about giving up ballet. She hadn't looked forward to telling her, and Moth's uncompromising attitude tore the scab off her hurt and made her want to strike back. 'Get on and be a great dancer if you're so good,' she said unkindly, 'but mind you don't fall off

24

your precious pointes. You're so stuck up you can't see where you're going.'

'I'm not, I'm not.' The taunt stung. 'Take your beastly shoe and don't be late for your lesson. You don't want to lose your place in the chorus.'

She held the shoe just out of Ruth's reach and then, as a group of girls on their way to the tap class appeared, thrust it into her hand. Ruth ran off to join the others, leaving Moth angry and alone.

She dawdled her way home, dragging her feet through gutters of dead leaves and stopping to speak to strange cats. She missed Libby's quick march to the tune of 'I'm starving, what's for tea', but more than she missed Libby, she missed Ruth and the endless conversations in which they always talked over the day. 'Wasn't it funny when Miss P. said . . . Trust Jane to have seen Baryshnikov . . . Who's that fair boy in the fourth year, the one who looks Swedish . . . ' It was a chance to pick up and sort out the fragments of gossip that made up their world, and it was so absorbing that often the two of them would stand for half an hour at the corner where their ways parted, unable to separate because there was still more to tell.

But today Moth arrived home early, so early that her great-aunt remarked on it.

'The others stayed behind for their tap class,' Moth explained, and then added resentfully, 'Ruth's given up ballet and gone over to tap.'

'Ruth, that's the plump little girl with the lovely smile?'

'I don't think there's anything special about her smile,' said Moth crossly. 'She used to be so keen on ballet, and good at it, and now, suddenly, she's dropped it and says I'm stuck up.' The accusation rankled as much as Ruth's desertion.

'She may have her reasons,' said her great-aunt gently.

'Well, what are they?'

'She may not want to tell you, especially if she's upset. Some people are like Libby and cheerfully blurt everything out, but others are more sensitive and keep their hurts to themselves. Perhaps she's been told that she's getting too tall or too fat. There's a right shape for dancers, isn't there?'

'Yes,' agreed Moth, 'and for dancers' feet.' She didn't want to find an excuse for Ruth, a reason that suggested she might have been hasty in quarrelling with her. She pushed Ruth to the back of her mind and turned instead to dancers' feet, explaining to her great-aunt that they needed to have the first three toes much about the same length and strong ankles. They were busy studying Moth's feet and trying to decide if they seemed all right when Libby arrived home.

'The lesson was marvellous,' she gasped, breathless after bounding up the stairs. 'We did simple taps in front and to the side, like this, and then you have to do a kicking movement.' She demonstrated.

Moth turned away, determined not to give her any encouragement. But Libby refused to be squashed.

'Apparently every year,' she said, punctuating her words with taps, 'the class supplies dancers for a pantomime. It's a proper one, so you get real stage experience, and this year they want two groups of six dancers. Although I'm only a beginner, I might get chosen because you have to be a certain height and have lots of personality. And I'm sure I've got that,' she added, with a grin.

'Well you're certainly not too modest,' said Great-Aunt Marion. 'If they need a spare trumpeter, you're very good at blowing yours.'

Moth couldn't laugh. She knew that she ought to be

26

glad for Libby's sake, but it was hard to be generous and encouraging when, without realising it, Libby looked like achieving her secret ambition. Although Moth had danced at festivals and in the shows put on at the school the previous year, she had never appeared in a real theatre before a paying audience. True, Libby would not be dancing in a ballet, but that didn't really matter. She had a chance – and knowing Libby she would seize the chance – of being involved in a professional performance. And, as though to punish Moth, the chance was provided by tap.

3

Out of step

It looked like being Libby's term. Everything went well
for her. She had a natural flair for tap and modern
dance, she was almost certain to be in the pantomime
and, what Moth found hardest of all to bear, she was
easily the best at ballet.

Miss Pearson was a demon for work, and kept everyone at full stretch. Moth felt she had never concentrated so hard before. There was so much to remember,
so many details that had to be combined to produce
movements that seemed effortless. It was all very well for
Miss Pearson to stress the importance of balance and
say that lack of it produced strain. It was so easy to put
one's weight in the wrong place, to have it too far back
so that it ruined one's arabesque and pirouettes, and
remarks like 'the arms have a different texture from the
legs', though they sounded helpful and Moth thought
she saw what Miss Pearson was getting at, were difficult
to translate into positions and movements. 'Placing,'
said Miss Pearson, 'is the foundation of ease', but some
days Moth felt that she couldn't place her head, or her
shoulders, or her arms, or her hips, or her legs, or her

28

feet correctly. And as for remembering that her arms had a different texture from her legs . . .

Libby, however, didn't need to think. Her arms and legs usually fell into the right position, and when a movement or a pose did have to be corrected, she seemed able to translate Miss Pearson's comments instinctively. She was also apparently tireless, bouncing home after her extra classes with undiminished energy.

She walked home with Ruth, who had ignored Moth since their quarrel. They didn't sit next to each other any more or seek each other out at break, and Moth now found the day disagreeably full of free time. There was no longer any point in arriving early so that she and Ruth could start the day with a good gossip, and she found herself wandering aimlessly round the classrooms at break because she didn't want to join up with anyone else. And after school there was nothing to do but go home to her great-aunt.

It was strange to feel so lonely when much of the day she was surrounded by the chattering mob of the rest of the class, but everyone else already seemed to have their own special friends, and there was no one with whom Moth felt in sympathy.

There was time, as there had never been time before, to read, and at last Moth got down to the books that had been sitting neglected on her bookshelf. They had mostly been given to her as presents, chosen because the givers had enjoyed them when they themselves were children or, Moth discovered, because they were about children who wanted to go on the stage. She read her way avidly through *Ballet Shoes* and the Noel Streatfeild books about Gemma. Her own discovery was a series of books about a group of children who called themselves the Blue Doors and formed their own theatre company. She had come across them in the public library, where the title *The Swish of the Curtain* caught her eye, and as the grey wintery term wore on, she found herself going there more and more often. It was something to do on the way home, and she could take out her restlessness on the books, discarding one after the other in her search for something that suited her lonely, irritable mood.

She was feeling particularly miserable one day at the end of October. It was the day of Ruth's birthday party, to which Libby and the rest of the class had been invited. Libby had made no secret of the invitation, though she knew Moth wasn't going. As she told her great-aunt, who tactfully said nothing to Moth, as well as lots of super food they were going to have fireworks.

Moth adored fireworks. No matter what it said on the box, each one was a surprise, because you never knew how far it would shoot, how loud a crack it would make, how long the fire would rain down, and you could never slow it down or make it stay a moment longer than its brief life. She always wanted more, and the fact that her father grumbled about money going up in smoke made them even more desirable! She loved dazzle, display, excitement, and firework parties offered all this.

So not being asked to the party was a double blow. She knew they were planning to have a bonfire and cook sausages and jacket potatoes in the ashes, and she could almost taste their smoky tang and see the faces gathered round the blaze. It's not fair, she thought. I would have enjoyed it so much and Ruth and I were real friends, not like Libby, just someone she knew.

She had thought of trying to make up the quarrel, but she wasn't sure how to go about it. She tried to imagine telling Ruth she was sorry, but the words wouldn't come and she felt shy and embarrassed. After all, Ruth didn't seem to be missing her, so perhaps she didn't want Moth as a friend. They didn't share class any more, so perhaps Ruth would rather have someone who shared her new involvement with tap. And I could never do that, thought Moth firmly. But she knew that because of her refusal to admit that she might have been hasty, if not altogether wrong, she was the loser. And not only because of the party. They had found the same things funny, Ruth was always having good ideas, and in Ruth's home Moth had glimpsed a world that she needed.

The others in her class didn't talk about the party in her hearing, but she sensed how much they were looking forward to it and the thought of seeing them all set off together became unbearable. The last lesson of the afternoon was a class, and as she slipped away to fetch her things, Moth knew that she wasn't going back. She felt reckless and disobedient. Miss Pearson would be furious, but Moth was in a mood to hurt herself. Yet once she was outside the school, she didn't know what to do. She saw the library as a refuge from the cold, unsympathetic streets, but she found herself looking resentfully at the shelves. Everything seemed to be out. There was nothing she wanted to read. She suddenly felt too old for the books in the junior section and decided to explore upstairs. It occurred to her that the adult library would probably have a shelf of books on ballet, and she set out to find them. She felt too shy to consult the girls on the information desk, and so she wandered around trying to work out how librarians classified ballet. It was plainly not under anything as simple as B. All the books were arranged by curious decimal figures and under unlikely categories, and she felt dazed by the sheer volume of knowledge. She was just about to give up – what else could one expect of a dead-end afternoon? – when a voice broke into her isolation.

'You've grown up very suddenly,' it said. 'What are you doing among all these weighty tomes?'

It was a voice from her first term in London, when she had met Robert Weston in the queue outside Covent Garden and he had befriended her. He was the eternal student, supposedly doing research for a book on nineteenth-century theatre which, he was the first to admit, would probably never be finished. He haunted libraries, somehow managing to spirit away enough books for half a dozen readers.

'I didn't want any of the books downstairs,' said Moth.

'And you don't much like the look of any of the ones upstairs, judging by your expression,' said Robert. 'You look fed up. I know that feeling only too well. You feel as though you'd like to kick the books because you're miserable and they're not prepared to do anything to help. Right?'

'Right,' agreed Moth.

'Well, if you hang on a minute while I get organised, I'll walk you home and you can tell me all your troubles. I don't suppose I can do anything to help, but it sometimes makes you feel better just to get things off your chest.'

Robert gathered up an armful of books, staggered to the checkout, and produced a pack of plastic tickets. The girl photographed them without comment, and Robert crammed the books into an ancient brief case and an old army haversack. 'I hate public libraries,' he confided to Moth, 'but I can't do without them. I can't promise to love and cherish a book for three weeks and then bring it back. I never know when I'm going to need it, whereas librarians see a book as something you read through and then hand back. But then they don't write books, they just enjoy cataloguing them.'

'But if everyone was like you,' said Moth, remembering the argument always put forward by her mother when she wanted to do anything anti-social, 'there

wouldn't be any books left in the library for other people to borrow.'

'But everyone isn't like me,' said Robert triumphantly. 'I want something different out of life from most people. And I thought you did too. What's become of all that ambition to be a great dancer?'

So Moth told him how sour the term had become. How she had quarrelled with her best friend, how Libby was certain to appear in a real show before she was, how her dancing wouldn't come right, and how the whole idea of ever becoming a dancer seemed so far away and impossible.

Robert listened. That was the great thing. He strode along beside her, weighed down by books, his face disappearing into the coils of his college scarf, a serious student who, flatteringly, was really listening to what she was saying, not as her parents or her great-aunt might have listened, but as though he were her age, or she his, and as though her problems were important.

'It seems worse,' he said, when at last she came to the end of her woes, 'because it's several things all at once. Life's like that. It seems to go in winning streaks or periods when everything goes wrong. But it won't last. You have to hang on and tell yourself that when things are really bad, they can only get better. They often don't seem to, or not at first, but already, far off, the wheel of fortune is beginning to turn in your favour, though it may be a while before you get any benefit.'

Moth was unconvinced, though she wanted to believe Robert. 'Do you think I shall be friends with Ruth again?' she said.

'Perhaps. But it's not as straightforward as that. You don't always get what you want in the shape you want it. But you must keep cool and make sure that you're able to take advantage of any good luck that comes your way.'

'How do I do that?' Moth was sure she knew far better than fate what would be best for her.

'Well, in your case, by concentrating on your dancing. At the moment, it's the thing you're best at, even if you are going through a sticky patch. It may lead somewhere, it may lead nowhere, but it's worth plugging away at it until something turns up. That's what I tell myself about my book, though I often feel it's not worth finishing because no one will want to publish it anyway.'

'Oh, I'm sure they will,' said Moth loyally.

'Maybe. But I know I'd rather be a failed writer doing something I enjoy, than stuck in an office which I know I'd hate.'

The afternoon had made rapid strides towards dusk, and shreds of mist blurred the street corners and the sharp outlines of the autumn hedges. The lights were on in most of the houses, but in many rooms the occupants hadn't yet drawn the curtains.

'They're like stage sets, aren't they,' said Robert, as they looked into a room lined with books where a man sat reading before an open fire. 'I love going out for a walk on a winter's night, especially when it's raining, and savouring the contrast between the chill outside and the warmth and comfort within.'

'Do you wish it was your home?'

'Sometimes. But in an odd way I enjoy the freedom of being outside. I love the elements, and the wind and the rain make me feel that I'm really alive, with everything ahead of me. Life ought to sting and be full of surprises, though for most people it's all too predictable. That's what attracts me about the theatre.'

Moth thought about this. Did she want to be a dancer just because it was such an uncertain, dangerous way of life? Certainly she longed for excitement and change, but would she be able to cope with a world governed by quite different rules from her safe background?

Now the darkness seemed threatening and hostile. She was glad of Robert's company even though she found his ideas uncomfortable. 'I'm sure Great-Aunt Marion will want to see you again,' she said, as they reached home and Robert passed the gate. 'I'll ask her if you can stay to tea.'

To console her for missing the party, her great-aunt had prepared her favourite tea: scrambled eggs on crumpets. Robert agreed that it was a delicious combination, and new to him. 'It's something I could do myself,' he said, providing a sudden glimpse of the way he lived. 'I share a gas-ring and a gas-fire with another mad student and our speciality is things on toast. He opens the tins while I make the toast.'

Moth didn't like to ask if that was all he had to eat. She had pictured Robert living in glamorous freedom, accountable to no one, the way she would like to be one day. Now she saw that there might be drawbacks. Robert's bed-sit didn't sound comfortable and well-cared-for like her bedroom. He might not have to tell anyone where he was going, but he didn't come back to a real home with someone waiting to get a meal ready.

But he seemed cheerful enough, and by the time Libby arrived home Moth found that she was feeling better. The party had obviously been fabulous, but it was over, and the hurt was over too. She was even able to listen to Libby's account of the fireworks and how Daniel had then made his own fireworks on the piano. She had forgotten about missing class too, until she and Libby were cleaning their teeth.

'By the way,' said Libby, in between gargling with unnecessary ferocity, 'where were you this afternoon?

Miss P. was very annoyed. She asked me to tell you that she wants to see you tomorrow, first thing. Rather you than me. She had that firm look, the way she looks when she's about to point out that you're out of step with everyone else.'

4

Mice, mermaids and Chinamen

Moth hated going to the staff-room. You knocked, you waited outside, the person you wanted never answered the door, and everyone who went past stared at you with a mixture of curiosity and sympathy, because a summons to the staff-room usually meant trouble.

But this morning Miss Pearson came to the door and stepped outside at once. 'Just the person I want to see,' she said briskly, 'but it's too cold to hang around here. Let's see if we can find an empty classroom.'

Moth was puzzled. What was there to say that would take that long? Was Miss P. going to give her a lecture? She jumped in quickly and began her explanation while Miss Pearson settled herself on the window sill near the radiator.

'I'm sorry I missed class yesterday, but I didn't feel well enough to come.' She thought of adding that she had felt faint, but it was probably better not to go into details.

Miss Pearson was unexpectedly sympathetic. 'Do you usually have a bad time,' she said, 'or was this an exception? I know the cold weather can sometimes make period pains feel a lot worse.'

Moth realised that Miss Pearson had come to an understandable conclusion about the cause of her absence, but it was not only untrue but so far impossible. Yet she hesitated to explain this, partly because it embarrassed her to talk about it and partly because it was a sign of growing up and she didn't want to be treated like a child. It had happened to Libby, and would presumably happen to her too, soon.

'No, I usually feel all right,' she said, blushing.

Miss Pearson looked thoughtful. 'I know period pains can be agony,' she said, 'and some people get them far more acutely than others. The reason I wanted to know is because I've been asked at very short notice to find a couple of extra dancers for a Christmas production of *The Nutcracker* ballet. The company put it on in London every year, and the children are always supplied by the same school and taught by an old friend of mine. This year, for some reason, she's had problems finding the right number of suitable children. The boys are always harder to find, so she wants to take a look at Tom, but now one of the girls she picked has hurt her foot and won't be able to dance. She thought I might have someone here who could take over, and she needs someone who's the right height and can pick up the steps quickly. I wondered if you would like to be considered?'

Would she! The question was so casual, as though it didn't matter much, but Moth was dazzled. She felt as though a flash bulb had exploded and caught Miss Pearson in her yellow practice dress and shapeless sweater outlined against a grey, unpromising sky.

'But it would be a drawback if you're inclined to feel rotten for a couple of days. There are a lot of rehearsals to fit in, and then you'd have to be available for a three-week season in the Christmas holidays. It's very hard work, and if you don't feel up to it, now's the time to say.'

I'll never tell another lie, never ever, Moth promised herself, if only I can have this chance. 'I've never felt ill before,' she said, truthfully, 'and I never get colds or anything like that. I'm sure I'll be all right.'

Miss Pearson smiled. 'O.K. Well I'll run you over to see Miss Wren this afternoon, but don't get too excited yet.' She had noticed Moth's shining eyes. 'I shall be taking Karen and Jane along too, and it'll be up to Miss Wren. It won't be my choice, but hers.'

There wasn't much room on the back seat of the Mini. The three of them were nervous and tense, aware of each other as rivals. Karen, who had been to auditions before, knew what it felt like to be turned down. Jane, who was used to getting her own way, expected to be chosen. Moth wished that she was wearing her silver dancer necklace. She believed in lucky charms and was tempted to play a silly game that she had invented. It went, if we get through the traffic lights before they turn red, it means that I shall get the part. She was relieved when Miss Pearson distracted her by asking if any of them had seen *The Nutcracker*.

Nobody had, not even Jane, who had usually seen everything. 'Daddy wouldn't take us,' she explained, 'because it isn't on at Covent Garden and he says it's not worth seeing an inferior production.'

'You won't be too popular if you say that at the audition,' said Miss Pearson. 'And if your family feel the production is so inferior, I'm surprised they're willing to risk you being in it.'

For once Jane didn't have an answer, and the others tried not to look too pleased. Serve her right. Moth decided that she wouldn't mention that she had once done a solo to the tinkling little dance of the Sugar-Plum Fairy. Everyone had said she was marvellous and ought to become a dancer, but they hadn't known what was involved. And in those days, neither did she.

'You'll probably recognise some of the music anyway,' said Miss Pearson. 'It's irresistible, and it's the main reason why the ballet is still performed all over the world even though the story is rather feeble. Various choreographers have tried to improve this by introducing new characters and pyschological interpretations, but the original ballet, which was first staged at St Petersburg in the time of the great ballet-master Petipa, was based on a Christmas story for children. It begins with a Christmas Eve party in the house of the Stahlbaums, who have two children called Clara and Fritz.'

'Are we auditioning for them?' asked Tom.

'No. They're important parts that will be danced by the stars of the company, but you might get a chance to be one of the other children at the party. There are several of them, as well as lots of other guests, and they get presents from the Christmas tree and dash round the stage getting in everyone's way. Then an eccentric, elderly gentleman called Dr Drosselmeyer arrives, and he brings Clara a very special present: a doll in the shape of a nutcracker.'

'Is it a real doll, or is it played by a dancer?'

'Well, it's a real doll to start with, though in the original version it later turns into a prince, and it soon causes trouble, because Fritz, who is jealous of Clara, snatches the doll away from her and manages to break it.'

'Just like a brother,' said Moth with feeling, remembering how often she and Toby had fought over presents.

'Dr Drosselmeyer mends the doll and later, when all

the guests have gone home and the children are supposed to be in bed, Clara steals back to the drawing room to fetch the Nutcracker. And then the clock strikes midnight and the magic takes over, apparently orchestrated by Dr Drosselmeyer. Everything that follows happens in a dream, and it begins with the Christmas tree growing taller and taller.'

'Do you see it grow?' asked Tom, and added, being very practical, 'How do they do it?'

'I'm not sure, but it certainly grows. It's one of the moments I enjoyed most when I was a child.'

'What else happens in the dream?' Moth was anxious to know what other parts there were, as well as the children at the party.

'The drawing room is suddenly invaded by mice and rats, and there's a tremendous battle between them and some toy soldiers led by the Nutcracker, who has now come to life. Clara saves him by throwing her slipper at the Rat-king, and as a reward the Nutcracker turns into a handsome prince and takes Clara on a journey to the Kingdom of Sweets. They pass through an enchanted forest full of whirling snowflakes, and the second act takes the form of a grand entertainment staged by the sweets in their honour. There's a Spanish dance, an Arabian dance, a Chinese dance, one of those Russian dances done by leaping Cossacks, a dance by the Old Woman Who Lived in a Shoe with all her children, and the famous Waltz of the Flowers. The dances are meant as a showcase for the talents of the company, and the final stars are the Sugar-Plum Fairy and her partner. And then at the end Clara wakes up and realises it has all been a dream.'

Moth still wasn't sure where they came in, but there wasn't time to ask. Miss Pearson had spotted a free meter and swooped joyfully into the precious space.

Then they were hurrying along corridors echoing with familiar sounds. 'Get changed quickly,' she whispered, shepherding them into the corner of a studio where a handful of girls were getting ready for a class.

The class was given by a small, dark-haired woman who flashed them a quick smile of welcome and then got on with the usual routine of bending and stretching exercises, first at the barre and then in the centre of the room. She paid no special attention to the newcomers, but Moth sensed that she was nevertheless assessing them with the shrewdness of an examiner. When they tried out their pirouettes, she showed them how to flick round. 'Your bottom half is your engine, and your top half must be all lightness, so that the engine doesn't have to work too hard. Good. That's right. You've got it,' she said to Moth as she spun round.

Moth was exhilarated by this encouragement and thought how well Miss Wren suited her name. She had the swift movements of a bird and a watchfulness that now and then gave way to a quick smile. Her commands were clear and decisive.

'Now that everyone's warmed up, let's have a shot at the Chinese dance. I assume that you four know the story' – they nodded – 'but you may not have worked out what parts we play. Boys and girls do the children in the opening scene, then the girls do the mice who creep in to steal the sweets when Clara falls asleep and the mermaids who dance round the boat in which she journeys to the Kindom of Sweets, then boys and girls do the Chinese dance while the mermaids change into the children of the Old Woman Who Lived in a Shoe. So you're on and off all the way through.

'For the Chinese dance, you have to imagine that you're very serious, rather prim mandarins. You shuffle on in pairs nodding earnestly away to each other and

43

then perform a formal little dance. The dance is in the shape of a square, so you need to spot each other and make sure that you keep the shape of the pattern. The men form the corners of the square and they have to stump round like this' – she showed them – 'with their feet splayed out. I'm two Chinamen short at the moment, so I want you to watch the others very closely and then see if you can join in.'

The music came from a cassette recorder and was a slender little tune piped by flutes. Moth concentrated on the link between the steps and the music. She realised that Miss Wren would want someone who could fit in as quickly as possible, and she was determined to take advantage of her photographic memory.

Tom was an instant success as a Chinaman. He pursed his lips into an inscrutable expression and bobbed round with his feet in a good second position. Miss Wren was plainly delighted.

Moth watched the other two anxiously. Karen was indistinguishable from the other girls until she turned the wrong way, but Jane, who couldn't seem to manage an oriental expression, nodded away as though her head was loose. Moth, who came last, got through the dance without a mistake.

'Well done. Now let's see how you shape up as mice. This is a test of your acting ability too, because you must make the audience feel the astonishment of a couple of greedy little mice who suddenly come upon an enormous box of sweets. I want to see your whiskers twitching in anticipation and your paws trembling with pleasure.'

They watched two experienced mice mime the scene and then tried to imitate them. Moth found it easy to imagine she had paws and whiskers and scampered realistically across the room, but Jane was too elegant and

44

made a comically well-bred mouse who looked far too superior to go scavenging.

While they were changing to go home, Miss Pearson and Miss Wren were obviously discussing them, and when they shook hands with Miss Wren she thanked them for coming and told Tom she hoped he'd be just as lively in the opening scene. He had definitely got the part, and looked as delighted as a greedy mouse. The three girls were given no clue as to which of them had been chosen, and Miss Pearson started the car and turned homeward before she gave them the answer.

'It wasn't an easy choice,' she said, 'because you all did well and I was proud of you. I'm only sorry that two of you have to be disappointed but, as Karen knows, this is one of the risks of auditions when there's only one part. Miss Wren has chosen Moth, but there will be other opportunities for you to take part in a ballet later on, because...'

Moth wasn't listening. She sat back in the darkness and happiness exploded inside her like a firework. She'd done it. She was going to dance in a real ballet.

She came down to earth to hear Jane saying, 'I don't mind at all, Miss Pearson. In a way I'm rather glad. I don't think my parents would like me to make my debut disguised as a mouse or a Chinaman.'

Liar, thought Moth, trying not to giggle. She was surprised how determined and confident she suddenly felt.

5

Rehearsals

Miss Pearson dropped Moth at the corner of her road and she danced the rest of the way home. She saw the houses as a series of brilliantly lit stages cut out in the darkness and whirled her way past them, her feet flashing on the pavement. She didn't bother to shut the gate, dug impatiently in her pocket for the key, and then soared up the stairs in flying leaps.

'Guess what,' she shouted, 'guess what's happened, Great-Aunt Marion! I'm going to dance in a real ballet!'

They had finished tea long ago. Great-Aunt Marion was in her armchair reading, while Libby was draped over the settee doing her homework. Moth's words were like a shower of sparks that was suddenly extinguished.

'What's the matter?' she said uneasily. 'Aren't you glad?'

'You're very eager to tell us now,' said her great-aunt, looking up from her book, 'but I suppose it didn't occur to you that you ought to have let me know that you would be late home. As it is, I had no idea what had become of you, and neither had Libby. I rang the school, and they didn't know. Libby rang several of her friends to see if they had seen you or knew where you were, and I've been trying to decide whether to ring your parents or the police. And now you come in shouting about being in some ballet and aren't we glad. It's too bad of you, and if it means that you're going to be out all hours and I'm never going to know where you are, then you're certainly not going to be in any ballet.'

'I'm sorry,' murmured Moth in a subdued voice, 'but I completely forgot about letting you know. It was all so exciting and we were in the car with Miss Pearson so I knew we'd be safe, and I forgot that you wouldn't know about it. I'm truly sorry. I didn't mean to upset you.' She knelt down in front of the armchair and tried to put her arms round her great-aunt.

But her body remained stiff and unrelenting. Moth could smell the spicy fragrance imparted by her old-fashioned brand of soap and toilet water, but there was none of the soft warmth she was used to in her mother.

'You don't understand,' said her great-aunt with a sigh, 'but I'm beginning to feel that I'm too old to take on the responsibility of two young people. It isn't good for me to be worried like this. I didn't realise when I offered to have you both here that it would mean more than just providing you with a home in term time. I didn't foresee that you'd want to be involved in things, things that need the kind of support I can't give.'

Moth was shocked and dismayed. She tried again to hug her great-aunt and insisted, 'But you've given us a lovely home. We're not complaining.'

'Oh but you are, though you don't see it like that. You want to be out doing things. Libby wants to audition for a pantomime and now you want to be in this ballet. How are you going to get to the theatre every night? You're too young to be out late by yourselves, and I'm too old to be able to escort you.'

Moth didn't know what to say. If only they all lived in London her mother would be able to run her round in the car, as the other mothers did. No one else, she thought wistfully, was dependent on an elderly great-aunt. She had been so swept away by the possibility of appearing in the ballet that she hadn't thought about the consequences. She wondered whether Miss Pearson might be willing to give her a lift, but this evening had been a special occasion.

'Well, you must be hungry by now,' said her great-aunt, 'I'd better go and get you some supper.'

So far Libby had said nothing and had apparently been calmly getting on with her homework. Now, as soon as her great-aunt had left the room, she sat up and announced, 'If I get chosen, I'm going to take part. I shall find someone to take me to the theatre, and if I don't, I shall go on my own, whatever she says.'

Moth couldn't get to sleep that night, not even when she had curled up into a ball and pulled the sheet over her head. She was warm and safe, but her mind refused to shut down. Instead, it kept thrusting scenes before her as though it was sorting through a pile of slides. The Christmas tree wouldn't stop growing. The mice were attacking the Chinamen. She was in the wings but couldn't reach the stage. There must be a way, she said desperately, and like Libby, I must find it. But it was all part of her dream.

Miss Pearson asked Moth and Tom to stay behind after class.

'Now that we know you've got the part,' she said cheerfully, 'I expect you'd like to know what you've let yourselves in for.'

4

Moth tried to recapture her enthusiasm, but it was clouded by difficulties.

'The company will be putting on *The Nutcracker* for three weeks after Christmas, opening on Boxing Day, and there'll also be a two-week tour beforehand, at the beginning of December. You won't be taking part all the time, because there are two casts and each of you goes on tour for a week and divides the time in London. You all rehearse together, with rehearsals twice a week after school and a couple of full run-throughs with the company before the tour. I shall be sending your parents a letter explaining exactly what's involved, but have either of you any questions?'

'Do we get paid?' asked Tom eagerly.

'Yes, but I'm not sure how much. I don't think it's a fortune, so don't make any extravagant plans.' She noticed that Moth was looking despondent. 'What's up with you, you don't look too happy.'

'My parents don't live in London, and my great-aunt is worried about the arrangement. She hasn't got a car and she says she's too old to keep taking me to rehearsals. How am I going to get there?' She didn't want to make too much of the problem, in case Miss Pearson decided it would be easier to use Karen or Jane.

'We've got a car,' said Tom helpfully, 'and my mother will be taking me. Moth could come with us.'

Moth's one encounter with Mrs Blundell-Smith had not been a happy one, as she had been under the impression that it was Moth's fault that Tom had been injured in a skateboard accident. Moth remembered her as a large, overbearing woman who idolised Tom and always said the wrong thing in a very loud voice. Still, she would cheerfully put up with that if it solved the problem.

'I'll see what I can do,' promised Miss Pearson. 'I expect something can be worked out.'

And so it was. Mrs Blundell-Smith, overjoyed that her treasure was to appear in a proper production – 'not one of those horrid pantomimes full of nasty innuendoes' – was quite willing to find room for Moth in a car that, like its owner, was built on generous, rather showy lines. She made Moth feel like an extra parcel from Harrods, but at least she was a parcel that Mrs Blundell-Smith was prepared to call for and return to its rightful owner. And there was no doubt that she enjoyed saying graciously to Great-Aunt Marion, when she thanked her for bringing Moth home, 'Don't mention it, Miss Graham, it was my son's idea. He's so thoughtful.'

Tom was greatly enjoying himself as one of the more unruly children in the opening scene. He had to dash round the stage with a toy engine, gather round Dr Drosselmeyer while he opened his trunk full of presents, and watch the fight between Drosselmeyer's nephew, Karl, and Hermann von Rattenstein, an arrogant young man who also had his eye on Clara's elder sister, Louise.

Moth had to make her entrance through the fireplace, and then she and a girl called Nadia ran into the middle of the stage, sniffing the air inquisitively until they pounced on the sweets. As well as matching their steps to the music they had to memorise carefully where various items on the stage would be.

'You must be prepared to be adaptable,' warned Miss Wren, 'because even when you've practised on the actual set, you'll find that things can change position from one night to the next. Being a dancer isn't just a matter of dancing. You need to be able to make lightning adjustments.'

So far the rehearsals had been just like those for an ordinary school production. The first step into the world of a professional performance came when they were finally summoned to the company's studio.

It was a much grander room than any of them had practised in before, but it had in common with all studios a polished wooden floor, walls lined with mirrors, and the usual practice barres. They changed into leotards and woollen tights and Miss Wren insisted on cardigans, though everyone was too excited to feel cold. Then they tucked themselves into a corner to watch.

The scene was one of vivid confusion as the company began to arrive. They could not, thought Moth, as she tried to recognise some of the principals, ever be mistaken for anything but dancers. Although they were all basically in practice dress, the colours and variations were intensely individual. Leotards were just visible beneath chunky sweaters, tights disappeared into darned leg-warmers; some of the men wore track suits or baggy mackintosh pants, and T-shirts with slogans were very popular. Moth liked the ones that read To Live is to Dance, To Dance is to Live, and The Gobi Desert Canoe Club, and she noticed that a cheeky-looking boy with defiant curly hair had clearly labelled himself 'Bovver'.

The variety of dress was matched by a continual restlessness. Dancers, it seemed to Moth, never sat still. Some stood at the barre limbering up with the concentration of athletes. Some worked away at a problem movement, a turn, an arabesque that was somehow not right, studying their reflections in the mirror as though determined to find fault with their other self. Others had persuaded a partner to help, and spun round trying to correct a hold or a lift. Everywhere there was movement, chatter, contact, until suddenly the room was called to order by a decisive girl in a scarlet track suit. And, amazingly, the pattern of bodies shifted like the pieces in a kaleidoscope and *The Nutcracker* took shape.

Though at first it was hard to see the shape. The only

props were a few chairs and there seemed to be far too many people on stage. Several casts were rehearsing at once, so that many of the principals had a double who imitated their solo and then drifted back to rejoin the pack of stray dancers. Yet the shape was plainly clear to one man, the choreographer, a commanding figure in a striped shirt and striped trousers that reminded Moth of a deck chair. He was like a conductor with all the resources of an orchestra, bringing this dancer in, leaping forward to re-position that one, and every so often clapping his hands to halt the music.

This was provided by a pianist, for no tape recorder could have kept up with the constant repeats and calls to go back about half a dozen bars, let's take this entrance or that solo again. The dancers didn't spare themselves, but attacked their roles with a vigour that was the more effective because it was happening only a few feet away. And a particularly dashing solo, as when Fritz shot into the air with his legs out sideways, was greeted with appreciative applause.

Then it was the turn of the mice to dart on. Their quivering steps were not quite right and the choreographer was quick to show them just what he wanted. At one point Moth and Nadia had to jump across two kneeling rats, taking a step on their backs, and they practised this several times before scurrying away to watch the fierce battle between the rats and the band of toy-soldiers. The king rat had long blond hair, dark glasses, dungarees and tough boots, and looked as though he would be equally happy on a motor-bike. I wonder why people think male dancers are soft, thought Moth, after they had nearly been trampled on by a horde of athletic soldiers who threw one of the rats across the stage . . . and caught him.

If the men emphasised their strength and energy, the

54

girls, whatever their gear, were irresistibly feminine. They reminded Moth of deer, with their dark alert eyes intensified by pencil outlines, their small, slight features and slim, graceful figures. Some, presumably the principals, had an imperious manner, but in between dancing they too could be seen sewing ribbons on their shoes.

The time passed so magically that Moth was surprised when she saw that Mrs Blundell-Smith had tiptoed in with unusual tact and was regarding the scene with pride and fascination. True, she probably didn't approve of the tough young men, especially the one who openly proclaimed himself a Bovver, but she was reassured by the neatness of the children, the obvious vigilance of Miss Wren, and the presence of no less than two chaperons, who were knitting away amid a heap of parked cardigans.

'It's a wonderful experience for you both,' she commented later, as the car purred along in the middle of the road. Tom started to tell her how the soldiers did somersaults and the Russian dancers played leapfrog and shot their legs straight out in front of them while crouching down, but Moth sat silent and happy. There was nothing she felt able to say to Mrs Blundell-Smith, or to anyone else. She had been in a turbulent world that she found intoxicating, and the only sounds that might have expressed her joy belonged not to words but to music.

6

One of the cast

Libby's reaction to Moth's success was typical. She didn't bother about why Miss Pearson hadn't asked her to audition, or develop any doubts about her own ability as a dancer, as Moth would have done. She made up her mind to shine at tap and modern dance so that she would be chosen for *Sinbad the Sailor*, and she concentrated all her energy on that.

As with the children in *The Nutcracker*, much depended on height. They were needed as urchins, pygmies and monkeys, and for a sparkling dance on the shores of the Diamond Isle, and they were chosen by the choreographer, a tall, restless man in a red shirt and black braces who chewed gum when he wasn't pulling on a cigarette. He looked them over, sorted them into groups and sizes, lined them up, stepped back to see if he liked the view, and then nodded acceptance to Mrs Slade, who had once appeared in one of his shows.

'That looks O.K. to me, darling. I'd like them three or four times a week because I want them with the company in about a fortnight. Lorna will teach them the songs and help with the run-through. See you.' And he took off as though he had a jet to catch.

Of course he had chosen Libby, but she didn't rush home to tell Moth and her great-aunt. She listened attentively to the time-table of rehearsals and performances, which began just before Christmas and included Boxing Day, and she accepted that she would have to make her own travel arrangements.

The theatre was in a small town just outside London, and Libby foresaw all too clearly the objections that would be raised if she asked her great-aunt to cope with anything else. Despite Mrs Blundell-Smith's chauffeuring, she saw that her great-aunt found Moth's erratic movements unsettling, and she sometimes seemed too tired to respond to Moth's rapturous account of what this or that dancer did or how she had been praised by no less a person than the choreographer. Libby didn't want to add to the strain, but she had no intention of giving up the part.

I shall have to tell Moth, she thought, because she'll find out anyway, but I shall make her promise to keep it a secret for the time being.

'You'll never get away with it,' said Moth, when Libby explained her plan. 'She's bound to ask what you're doing when you stay behind to practise, and you can't possibly find a reason for staying out late every night.'

'I shan't need to by then. At first I shall say we've got extra classes, which is really true, and then once I've learned the part, I shall be so good at it that the choreographer guy won't want to do without me. I shall tell him about Great-Aunt Marion and how we haven't got a car, and he's bound to come up with a solution.'

'Like harnessing some mice to a golden carriage,' suggested Moth scornfully. Her mind tended to run on mice these days, and she kept trying out mouse faces in the bathroom mirror and seeing if she could make her nose twitch.

'There's a couple of Saturday rehearsals at the theatre,' Libby went on, ignoring Moth's sarcasm, 'and if we can get through those, it will be too late to replace me by anyone else. It'll mean being away all the morning, and I thought you could say that you were rehearsing and had asked if I could come along too see how a proper company practise.'

Moth was amazed by Libby's ingenuity and nerve. 'It sounds like an awful lot of lies,' she said, 'and I don't see why I should get involved. Great-Aunt Marion has a very strict idea of truth, and if there's any more trouble, she may decide she doesn't want us any more. And if we can't live here, we won't be able to stay at the school.'

It was this that really mattered, but Libby was in no mood to be deterred. 'You selfish pig,' she said, hammering the words into Moth. 'You've got what you wanted, and you know that it means just as much to me. Well if you don't help me, I'll make you sorry, and if you ever need any help in the future, I'll see you don't get it.'

And Moth knew she would. Libby was even more dangerous as an enemy than she threatened to be as an ally, and Moth didn't relish the idea of having to watch her step continually in case Libby spotted her opportunity and pounced.

'All right,' she agreed, 'but you've got to do the talking.'

'Sure,' said Libby confidently, 'just leave all the talking to me.'

And the plan worked. While Moth practised being a mermaid and whirling out of the Old Woman's shoe,

Libby at her 'extra classes' learnt the songs and dance routines of *Sinbad the Sailor*.

The day of the Saturday rehearsal began with a brilliant pale blue sky. They had to get to the theatre by train, and Libby agreed to finance the expedition from her savings. The train rattled past rows of houses with gardens running down to the line, before it reached a sort of compromise countryside. Here skeletal trees stood knee-deep in dead leaves, the bushes had scarlet berries, and the playing fields were a healthy winter green. The light was so clear you could see as far as a bird, and Moth was surprised by the speed with which her guilt dissolved as she began to enjoy the adventure. It was like being on holiday. When they arrived, even the station with its neat fretted boarding had a contented, countrified air.

They had to ask the way to the theatre and then only found it by chance, so inconspicuously had it been inserted into the high street. The foyer was already alive with activity. The box office was open and had customers, and the café was full of shoppers who had discovered the excellent coffee. Moth and Libby felt very professional as they walked past them and into the theatre itself, which at this hour was closed to the public.

It was a modern theatre, built of plain undisguised brick, and there were no circles or gallery but just a single level of steeply raked seats. Most of them were empty, but those in the front were occupied by an assortment of gear: jackets, sweaters, socks, tissues, scripts, Adidas holdalls crammed with theatrical junk.

Libby's group had gathered in the front two rows and were hopping around in a mixture of ballet shoes and plimsolls. They were stoking up their energy with bags of crisps and tubes of sweets while a harassed-looking older girl, who was trying to decide whether to train as a teacher, tried to sort them out and keep order.

She was glad to see Libby and not at all put out that Moth had come too. 'Perhaps you could keep an eye on our things while I show Libby where to change,' she said, and Moth promised to look after the possessions. It was reassuring to have something official to do.

She chose a seat and settled down to observe the company. They had in common with dancers a larger-than-life presence, as though they needed to project an image. And their clothes were part of this boldness. A pretty girl with tangled fair hair was wearing jeans and a white T-shirt sprinkled with gold glitter. A comic in a blazer had a coloured stripe down the side of his trousers as though he was a hotel pageboy. Languid youths and imperious girls in dungarees and baggy track suits lounged around the stage, and a serious young man with a fringe was working out a comedy routine with some-one half his size. They were impatient to start, waiting for a signal from the director, a tanned, balding man deep in conference with his aides. Moth sensed that it would be his job to turn a collection of individuals into a company.

She was surprised how seriously everyone took the rehearsal. Once it began, instead of walking through their parts, the cast performed as though they had an audience. Some of the lines needed an answer, as when the dame, Mrs Sinbad, played by the man in the blazer, was looking for his dromedary Drusilla. She was played by two men in a furry skin, and Moth could see them looking through a spyhole in the humps. Mrs Sinbad kept losing Drusilla, and the rest of the cast shouted out just like an audience 'She's over there,' as Drusilla skipped nimbly out of the way.

The opening chorus had to be adjusted to fit the stage, and the choreographer, this time dressed all in white,

60

would spring down the aisle and up on to the stage to work out the details of the routine. He would walk the steps, muttering the counts to himself, get the chorus to do it, and then check his positioning from the back row of the theatre, only to bound down again to correct the bell kicks or give the diagonal lines more emphasis. 'Take that arm out, now bring it back in as the other one goes out,' he chanted, dancing with them and occasionally thrusting a child into place.

Moth was glad that Libby seemed to be doing well. She overheard the director say, 'That child's got what it takes. The bright ones are always keen and alert and utterly immersed in what they're doing', and guessed he was talking about Libby.

She was caught up in the spirited battle beween the Old Man of the Sea, who hissed and cackled in a feast of over-acting, and the good fairy, who was released from a bottle fished up by Sinbad and spoke her verse in a low, dark voice that came from Africa. Even the love scenes, which were mostly songs about a man chasing a girl until she catches him, had a charm that transcended the bare stage, and Moth knew just how the heroine felt when she sang, 'I'd like to do the kind of things I've never done before'.

Then they broke for coffee, and Moth realised that it was exhausting and hungry work deputising for an audience. Libby of course was starving, and they queued up in the café with the rest of the cast while the public, as Moth now thought of them, stared at them with respectful curiosity. 'Cast?' asked the girl when it was their turn to pay, and Libby said firmly, 'Yes'.

When they went back to the auditorium Moth wandered up on to the stage. The set of the current play – a collection of white cubes designed to convey a stark modern office – was stacked at the back, and the wings were an alarming tangle of ropes and switches. Suddenly she came upon the young man with the fringe, who had folded himself out of sight in a corner to learn his lines. He was even younger and more serious close to, and she wasn't sure whether to speak to him – Libby would have done – so she smiled shyly, and he did too.

'You're very good,' she said, sensing that this was the right thing to say to an actor.

'Thanks.' He really did look grateful. 'This is my first pantomime, and I've never been a funny man before. But I've been out of work for nearly a year and then my agent came up with this.'

'What do you usually play?'

'Anything I can get nowadays, but I'm really a straight juvenile and I'd like to get into the RSC or the National. I've got some auditions coming up and my agent hopes to get me some television work.'

It was all only hopes, but Moth was impressed. 'I'll look out for you.'

'The worst thing about this part,' he said dolefully, 'is that I won't be able to get home for Christmas. I live up north and we've got a show on Boxing Day. It'll be the first time I haven't been able to get back to my family, and it's no fun spending Christmas in digs.'

'I'm going to be away from home too,' said Moth, but before she could tell him about *The Nutcracker* it was time to start again.

The choreographer produced a plan of the stage and explained that the Valley of Diamonds scene opened with the chorus in position amid piles of diamonds and behind a gauze that would rise for the diamond ballet. It was difficult to fit a ballet on to such a small stage, and the children and languid youths kept getting in each other's way. The timing was wrong, the arms were wrong, someone got lost. 'From the very top,' shouted the choreographer, twisting a child into place, 'and don't stick your bum out,' he yelled, as he leapt back to study the effect.

Now Moth discovered the boredom of rehearsals: the endless waiting around by the rest of the cast, the repetition necessary to get a number just right, the irritation and frustration, the inevitable routine of a life that needed an audience to get the adrenalin flowing.

By the end, when the exhausted cast gathered round for the director's candid comments, she had lost many of her illusions. The theatre was tough, tiring and, for long stretches, unbelievably dull.

Libby, however, was undiminished and undismayed. She took the repetitions in her stride, accepted that they would have to have an extra session on Monday, changed in a hurry, grabbed Moth and hissed, 'We must get to the station. We forgot to ask about the trains back.'

'Can't we just stop for something to eat,' pleaded Moth, recalling the appetising wholemeal rolls gaping with cheese that she had noticed in the foyer café. She also wanted to savour again the sense of being 'cast', of being on the inside of the profession.

Libby, for once the more farsighted, was reluctant, but she agreed that there were bound to be frequent trains going somewhere as important as London. So they sat around with rolls and fizzy orange, listening to the cast complaining or suggesting how to make improvements. Moth caught the eye of the fringed young man, who was trying to sort out a routine with his partner in crime, and he smiled and she smiled, as one performer to another.

When they finally got to the station they had just missed a train, and a surly official informed them that there wasn't another one for an hour.

'We shan't be home by tea time,' said Moth, appalled.

'Great-Aunt Marion will never believe I've been rehearsing all this time. She's bound to ring Tom's mother, and then she'll find out that we've lied. And it's all your fault,' she said bitterly, forgetting that Libby had wanted to come straight to the station. 'Just when everything was going so well, you had to spoil it.'

7

Stranded!

While Moth and Libby, cross, helpless and marooned, were quarrelling over who was to blame most, Great-Aunt Marion, far from wondering where they were, had settled down for her afternoon nap.

She had had a tiring morning shopping, and had had to make several trips because she was too proud to struggle along laden with plastic bags, but insisted on looking dignified and carrying an old-fashioned wicker shopping basket. She also refused to patronise super-markets, preferring a parade of little shops where, although things cost more, she knew the shopkeepers and they knew her and always exchanged a few words.

Her arthritis was worse in the winter and she was aware that it sometimes made her crotchety and irri-table. She disliked excuses and people who were always grumbling about their aches and pains, but it was diffi-cult to welcome the extra work caused by Moth's enthusiasm and Libby's restlessness.

'I haven't even asked Libby what happened about the pantomime,' she said to herself reproachfully. 'I suppose she wasn't chosen after all, but it was good of her not to make a fuss and to be prepared to watch Moth rehearse. They're both really very nice children.' She felt a sudden affection for them and decided they deserved a nice tea, especially as Libby had said something about a snack lunch.

She tried to remember exactly what Libby had said, but they had been in such a hurry to rush off that it had been rather confusing. They're bound to be hungry, anyway, she thought, as she called in at the bakers for a currant teacake with frosted sugar and indulged Libby's passion for cream doughnuts. They were made on the premises, as was all the bread, and while she was there, the baker, a burly Irishman, came through into the shop with a tray of seed rolls warm from the oven. She knew Moth loved their crisp little plaits so she bought some of them too.

After she had had lunch and done the washing up, she put the things ready for tea. Then she sat down with a book and slid gently off into her nap.

Meanwhile Moth and Libby were pacing the platform in gloomy silence. They had explored the station from end to end, walking out along the full stretch of the platform to the point where the station buildings began to look smaller and they could see into the signalbox. They tried the waiting room as a refuge from the biting air, but the cracked stone floor and scuffed seats seemed to be breathing out stale smoke. They read every advertisement until they could have passed an exam on the specialities of the local Indian restaurant, the advantages of an Awayday ticket, the current attractions at the Hippodrome and bargain holidays by British Rail. And still the train didn't arrive.

Moth kept imagining that she could hear it in the distance. She pictured it dawdling along the lines and

willed it to hurry up. But there was nothing in sight.

Libby had returned to the end of the platform, past the bookstall, the left luggage, the toilets, the carefully tended flowerbed sunk in its winter sleep, and was humming a song about opening a new window while she practised the opening routine. She accepted that there wasn't a train because, as yet, it wasn't due.

Great-Aunt Marion slept on. The afternoon closed in round the house and it was not light enough to read without the lamp. In the garden a tabby cat, tired of watching movements among the damp leaves, rubbed itself against a downstairs window and asked silently to be let in.

When at last the train arrived, it took the journey at a leisurely tempo as though it were out for a Saturday afternoon stroll. It stopped at every station for a friendly chat, waited while shoppers manoeuvred giant parcels on and off, stopped to watch a lusty pack in red and yellow jerseys slogging it out on a sports field, and finally expired to shouts of 'All Change'.

The station was flooded with passengers, none of whom seemed to know where to go. A distorted voice trying to be helpful only added to the confusion, and there was a feeling that the next train was about to go, was even at this moment slamming its doors, but from which platform?

Moth and Libby raced down the stairs into a subway and stood there uncertainly. Several platforms said London, but from which was the next train going? There was no one to ask. Just a tide of determined travellers who threatened to sweep them away.

'London?' shouted Moth at a young woman who was struggling with a child in a push-chair. But the woman only shook her head as the crowd moved her on.

'London?' yelled Libby, getting hold of a purposeful-looking man. But he wasn't going their way either.

Finally, they made their way to the ticket barrier where an official told them the right platform as though it was common knowledge and certainly not a matter of any urgency.

When Great-Aunt Marion woke up, she was surprised to see that it was a quarter to four. She switched on the lamps, drew the curtains to shut out the declining day, and began to worry. Surely the girls should be home by now? She tried to remember what Moth had said about the rehearsal, but most of the talking, as she recalled, had been done by Libby. The rehearsal was to be with the company, but how long would it take them to dance through *The Nutcracker*? A whole morning perhaps, but surely not half the afternoon too? I expect Mrs Blundell-Smith has asked them back to tea, she thought, but why haven't they rung up to tell me? Moth is usually a thoughtful child, even if Libby is rather wilful, and they must know that I shall worry. I think I shall ring up just to make sure, even if it does give the impression that I'm a fussy old woman. And she hunted for her glasses, which had slipped down the side of her chair, and went to look up Mrs Blundell-Smith in the directory.

'We must ring her up,' said Libby suddenly, 'and say that Tom's mother has asked us to tea. That would explain why we've been away so long.'

'It wouldn't work,' said Moth, 'because she'd hear the pips before we pressed the button and then she'd know we were ringing from a call box and not from Tom's.'

'Perhaps if we inserted the money before she
69

answered,' Libby suggested, 'we could get straight through. If she's going to find out anyway, surely it's worth a try.'

Moth couldn't be bothered to argue. It's her fault, it was her idea, she thought resentfully. She hated the way Libby never accepted restrictions, always fought against defeat, overriding Moth's scruples and faint-heartedness with her headstrong self-confidence.

'Well I think it's worth a try,' said Libby obstinately, but at that moment the train for London arrived.

Mrs Blundell-Smith was surprised by Great-Aunt Marion's call and not in the least reassuring.

'My dear Miss Graham, how terribly worrying for you. No, I'm afraid I've no idea where the girls are. The company rehearsal was yesterday, not today, and Tom hasn't said anything about any extra ones. And I'm sure he'd know. But if you hold on a moment I'll just check.'

Tom was safely watching some dangerous sport on television.

'Hullo, no, Tom is sure there are no rehearsals today. Where can they have gone? I don't want to alarm you, but if they're not back soon, perhaps you should ring the police. They do hear about accidents very quickly, I believe.'

When Great-Aunt Marion had finally silenced Mrs Blundell-Smith's offer of help and disturbing specula-tions, she sat by the telephone for a while thinking. They had obviously planned to go somewhere, not just dis-appeared, and she would surely have heard if one of them had had an accident. But supposing they had been picked up? She could imagine Libby being tempted by some adventurous offer. One read such extraordinary and terrible things in the papers. I'm too old for all this, she concluded wearily, I must hand back the responsibility to where it belongs.

And yet she was reluctant to take such a step. It hurt her pride to have to admit that she couldn't deal with the situation herself. She had always been such a capable, independent woman. During the war, no less a person than an admiral had complimented Wren Graham on being cool and resourceful – but that, she told herself wryly, was nearly forty years ago. I expect I'm getting to the age when I'm fit company only for other old ladies. But she didn't want to accept this. Moth and Libby were a worry and a lot of work, but they were worth it. Their energy, their enthusiasm, their noise, even those absurd hamburgers and chips and beans they were so fond of, jolted her, but it was a jolt in the right direction: towards life. And in hearing their plans, becoming aware again of terms and outings and parties, she had found that she was reliving her past, remembering what it was like to be young.

But the children were only on loan to her, and if they had come to any harm, further delay might be crucial. She could imagine people saying afterwards, 'Why ever didn't that great-aunt get help? She must have known she couldn't do anything by herself.' And so she picked up the phone and dialled again, and this time she called Moth's father.

The journey by tube across London was every bit as tiresome as that by the local train had been. Moth felt as though every foot of the journey had become a battle. The train was packed with rowdy football supporters, irritable shoppers, impatient weekend travellers, all caught up in an aggressive jollity that masked the underlying violence. By the time Moth and Libby reached home they felt too tired for explanations, let alone repercussions. Moth had been trying to think of what to say, how to begin, but it was Libby who hulloed up the stairs.

'Thank God you're all right,' said Great-Aunt Marion. She didn't look cross, as Moth had expected, but strained, unhappy and frail. 'No, don't tell me,' as Libby began to explain, 'I've sent for your father, Moth, and you can save your story for him. I've told him that I can't cope any more, and he's driving down to decide what should be done.'

8

Peace terms

How on earth, David Graham had asked himself as he put down the phone after trying to reassure his aunt, how on earth did I ever produce a child like this?

It was not the first time Moth had baffled him. He found the whole dancing business incomprehensible and couldn't see it as a worthwhile career. To him ballet was no more than an ornament, a kind of frivolity that he couldn't take seriously and that made him feel uncomfortable, with its handsome youths in tights, so obviously in love with themselves and so eager to show off their beauty. And he worried about its effect on Moth. It had taken her away from her family, so that she was growing up apart from them, and now apparently she had secrets, wanted to roam round London without telling her great-aunt where she was going.

It's no night to be a parent he told himself grimly, as he sped away from the dappled warmth of his own fireside and his headlights parted a fog that sealed impenetrably behind him. But it's not Marion's fault. Her help was a bonus, not something we had any right to take for granted, and it's a pity that wretched child doesn't realise that.

The 'wretched child' was waiting for him in her bedroom. Both she and Libby had gone to their rooms after a belated tea eaten in total silence. They made one or two attempts to talk to their great-aunt, but she didn't reply. She spoke only to ask if they wanted any more to eat, and the atmosphere of silent accusation was so intimidating that even Libby lost her appetite. There was obviously nothing to be said until her father arrived, and Moth was glad to escape to her room where the silence was just blank. She was shocked by her great-aunt's reaction, which seemed to her rather childish, and she couldn't understand why she was so upset. Why can't she see that Libby and I aren't likely to do anything silly or dangerous, she thought. If we were trusted more, we wouldn't need to do things without asking.

She decided to get undressed, and suddenly thought of cheering herself up by putting on her Japanese housecoat. It had been presented to her to celebrate her part in *The Nutcracker,* after Miss Wren had told them they would need something to wear in the dressing-room while making up and between performances. Most of the others would be bringing their dressing-gowns but Moth, who had only a blue woolly garment that had seen better days, had begged for something more glamorous.

'It looks so shabby,' she had wailed, 'and it's so old-fashioned. Some people have got proper housecoats with quilting and flowers. My dressing-gown's like Toby's and even the cord's all frayed.'

And it had been her great-aunt, she remembered guiltily, who had listened sympathetically to her and said that she might be able to find a solution. She had turned out one of the trunks in which were stored some old

75

family relics and unearthed a treasured but unused present that one of her brothers had brought back from the Far East years ago.

'I don't know why I never wore it at the time,' she said, unfolding the tissue paper in which it had been lovingly preserved. 'But I expect I thought it was too good to wear round the house and so I put it away for a special occasion that never turned up. But now' – she undid the last layer and revealed a splash of undimmed colour – 'I think the special occasion has arrived.'

The coat came from another world. It was made of scarlet silk and was of a simple design with wide sleeves and straight fronts held together by a tie belt. There was no question of size or fit: you just wrapped it round and tied it in place. Across the back sprawled a fierce dragon embroidered in black, silver and gold thread, and his smaller offspring coiled their way up the fronts. The embroidery was so vivid that the dragons seemed to be flashing their eyes and snorting fire from their nostrils as though they were glad that at last their long imprisonment was ended.

Moth was enchanted. She slipped the coat on and stood there, glowing. 'Can I really have it? Are you sure it's not still too precious to wear?'

Her great-aunt smiled. 'Well, perhaps it is, in purely commercial terms, but what's the point of keeping it and never using it? I was brought up to treasure things and take care of them, but one can hang on to things for too long. I'm sure you'll take care of it, and it looks just right for a dancer making her debut. I hope it will bring you good luck, my dear.'

Moth took the coat upstairs and hung it in her wardrobe. It shone as though it was alive, throwing out a challenge to the rest of her clothes. Now, as she took it out, she saw that it was an apt symbol of the theatre, a borrowed splendour that one put on.

It looked a little strange over her pyjamas, but it reminded her of the Chinese dance and she began to practise it, her bare feet enjoying the feel of the cool painted floorboards. As always, dancing soothed her, providing an escape from the uncertainties of the present.

The spell was broken by the arrival of her father. He had listened patiently to his aunt's side of the story and now he came, somewhat wearily, up to the attic to see what Moth had to say. But instead of finding a subdued, contrite child, he opened the door on a spirit who was flickering round the room like a leaping flame.

'What the hell are you doing?' he said irritably. 'Stop jigging about this minute and take that extraordinary thing off. I want a serious talk with you and I can't concentrate while you're dressed up like that.'

Moth subsided, took off the coat, and got out her old dressing gown. She felt extinguished, but her father obviously felt more at home with a blue woolly being. He sat down on the side of the bed while she pulled on a pair of socks and slipped her feet between the icy sheets.

'That's better,' he said. 'Now tell me what's been happening.'

And she told him, blaming Libby rather more than she had intended to, because it was really all her idea.

'But why didn't you tell us all this in the first place?' said her father. 'Can't you get it into your clever little heads that you can't solve these sort of problems by yourselves and that we can't help if we don't know what the problem is? I don't want to frighten you unnecessarily, but your great-aunt is getting old, and old people tend to get worried and upset more easily, and the results could be fatal. How would you and Libby have felt if

77

you'd arrived back to find that she had had a heart-attack?'

'We didn't mean to upset her . . . ' began Moth, but she was overtaken by tears. The coat blazed out from the wardrobe, reminding her of her great-aunt's loving generosity.

'No, I'm sure you didn't mean to hurt her,' said her father gently, 'but it isn't enough in life to mean well. You know it's wrong to tell lies and deceive people. It's taking too big a risk, don't you see?'

'But the theatre is about taking risks. How are Libby and I going to survive if we aren't prepared to be ruthless? Everyone says you have to be determined.'

'But you surely don't have to kill people to get on? Be determined, by all means, but use your brains as well. Your teachers, your great-aunt, us, we're all on your side, and if you had rung us up or told them at school about the difficulties, something could have been worked out for Libby, as I understand it has been for you. There was no need for you to intrigue like this.'

'What are you going to do?'

'At the moment, sleep on it. Your great-aunt has had a nasty shock and I can't insist that she lets you stay here. It will be up to her to decide whether she wants to go on with an arrangement that seems to be getting her down.'

'But I can't come home now!' Moth seized her father in protest. 'We're going on tour the week after next. It's all booked. I've learnt all the dances.'

'Maybe, but you don't seem to be learning how to be a nice person. Since you started to take dancing seriously, you've changed, and I'm not sure that I like the new Moth. Anyway, I've had enough for today. I think we'd all better sleep on it.'

78

'But daddy, please don't take away *The Nutcracker*, please,' begged Moth.

But her father refused to be drawn. 'We'll see,' was all he would say, 'we'll see how things look tomorrow.'

And with that he went downstairs to face a night on the sofa, while Moth tried to think of ways of winning round her great-aunt and Libby, the cause of all the trouble, slept soundly.

Moth knew what she was going to do as soon as she woke up. She lay for a few minutes cocooned in warmth, listening to the steady rain and the splash of a passing car. She didn't want to get up, but self-sacrifice was part of the plan.

She crept downstairs and glancing into the living room saw the untidy outline of her father jammed into the settee. He didn't look comfortable.

The kitchen came reluctantly to life as Moth switched on the electric fire and plugged in the kettle. Her great-aunt disliked the drying effect of central heating, which she said was bad for the furniture, and so each room was bracingly cold when it was not in use.

Moth took the butter out of the fridge and began to thaw it. She found an egg, some slices of bread, and the marmalade, and searched for one of the lacy cloths that she knew her great-aunt liked on a tray. It was to be a model breakfast, with a pot of tea, a jug of milk, a lightly boiled egg nestling under its cosy, a rack of toast and dishes of butter and marmalade. Moth was proud of her handiwork, which she felt would have been a credit to any hotel.

She was so determined to avert any catastrophe, that she wedged open the kitchen door and rehearsed the route to her great-aunt's bedroom to make sure that there weren't any unsuspected obstacles. Then balancing the tray very carefully she carried it to the room, knocked on the door the way she imagined they did in hotels, and went in.

The room was shadowy with sleep, but Moth edged her way to the bedside table and parked the tray on it. Then she twitched back the curtains, surprised by how dark it was outside, and said in her best maid's voice:

'Good morning, madam. Breakfast is served.'

It was some time before her voice had any effect on the figure in bed and then, instead of starting up to greet the day, it said sleepily:

'What's the matter? Whatever's the time?'

Moth had forgotten to look.

'I thought you'd like to have breakfast in bed for a change,' she said brightly, 'to make up for the rotten time you had yesterday.'

Her great-aunt tested the temperature of the air like a bather wondering whether to have an early morning dip. She tried reluctantly to sit up. Her white hair was secured in a schoolgirl plait and she was without her usual dignity.

'My watch . . . it's beside the bed somewhere. Tell me the time.'

Moth picked up the round watch and looked at its plain face. It said ten to seven.

'It's early,' she admitted, 'but you can have another sleep after you've had breakfast. And I'll get breakfast for the rest of us, so that you can stay in bed and read the paper.'

By now her great-aunt had struggled into a sitting position and was looking at the tray. Breakfast before seven was the last thing she wanted on a cold Sunday morning, but she was awake enough to realise that Moth meant well.

'Yes, I should like to stay put for a while,' she said

softly, finding just enough strength to pour herself a cup of tea, 'and I'm sure you and Libby are quite old enough to get yourselves breakfast.'

Moth wasn't sure whether she was being reproved or if this was the moment to speak out, but there was something she had to say.

'We do appreciate all you've done for us, really we do, and we didn't mean to give you a fright yesterday. If we hadn't missed the train, we wouldn't have been nearly so late, and Libby was going to tell you about the pantomime when we got back.'

Her great-aunt was drinking her tea as though she needed it to give her strength. Then she said, 'You only brought one cup, so I can't offer you some tea. Why don't you go and get another cup and fill up the pot while I pull myself together. You don't wake up so quickly when you're my age. It takes me a little time to get going.'

By the time Moth came back, her great-aunt had put on her bed-jacket and was much more wide awake. 'Curl up at the other end,' she said, and Moth tucked herself under the thick, quilted eiderdown. The satin felt cold, soft and slippery.

'I dare say you think I worry about nothing,' her great-aunt said, pouring them both a cup of tea, 'but we live in a dangerous world, and if you're fond of someone, you can't help being concerned. You don't see all the risks at your age, and I don't want to frighten you, but I can't accept that you're old enough to wander round London on your own.'

'But we can't become dancers without taking part in things, and it's not our fault that they happen in the evening and so far away. If you trusted us more, we wouldn't need to hide things, but Libby didn't tell you because she thought you'd stop her taking part.'

81

'Yes, I see that, but it makes me feel that I've taken on too much. This term has been much harder work than last year, and I suppose I've been too tired to cope. But if you felt you couldn't confide in me, why didn't you tell your parents about Libby?'

'Because they don't understand. Daddy's not all that keen on dancing, not really, and I suppose I was afraid that if it got too complicated, they might say it was more trouble than it was worth. But when they actually see me on the stage, they won't feel that, and if I've got *The Nutcracker*, it's only fair that Libby should have her chance too.'

In her earnestness Moth had pushed the eiderdown away from her. It seemed all wrong to be in bed at such a serious moment. She wanted to beg her great-aunt to understand how much it mattered, but they weren't dressed for the part and she had the feeling that her great-aunt was longing to go back to sleep.

'I don't think I feel clear-headed enough to work things out at the moment,' said Great-Aunt Marion. She was finding it difficult to get the top off her egg, which didn't seem as soft-boiled as Moth had intended. 'But I do see how important it is, and I want you to promise me something.'

'Yes.'

'You asked me to trust you, but it's really the other way round. If you'll trust me enough to tell me the problem, at least I'll have a chance to try and sort it out. And then if you think I'm being difficult, we can always ask your parents to referee.'

It sounded so easy, but Moth wasn't quite sure. She found herself sliding on to the floor, taking the treacherous eiderdown with her. She scrambled to her feet and suddenly felt very sleepy. 'I'll try, I promise, and now I think I'll go back to bed again, because I don't think Daddy or Libby will want breakfast yet.'

Later on it was Libby's turn to explain, and David Graham made her tell him exactly what being in the pantomime involved, how many performances she would have to take part in, and what was to happen over Christmas.

'Your great-aunt's not the only one who's been kept in the dark,' he said angrily, when the full extent of the Christmas upheaval became clear. 'Your mother's already disappointed that she won't be seeing much of you, even over Christmas, but it doesn't seem to matter much to either of you. Doesn't it occur to you that other people are involved. Toby and Lyn have as much right to enjoy Christmas as you two, but you're so wrapped up in this wretched theatre business that you don't seem able to think of anyone else.'

'We can take part though, can't we,' begged Moth, putting her arms round her father.

'It seems to be too late to do anything else.' He pushed her roughly away. 'But there will have to be conditions, and the conditions will have to be kept.'

So after a morning of discussions and phone calls the great Christmas plan gradually took shape. As Moth and Libby were both appearing on Boxing Day, they wouldn't be able to go home for Christmas but would have to stay in London with their great-aunt. The Graham family would drive up to London on Boxing Day and go with Libby to see the pantomime, while Mrs Blundell-Smith would be asked to take Moth to *The Nutcracker*.

'But you won't be able to see me dance,' said Moth, as the implications of the plan sunk in. 'You'll be miles away watching Libby.'

'Now don't start up again,' said her father, who prided himself on his skill as a negotiator and felt he had done well. 'It's the best we can do in the circumstances and it's not the only performance you're giving. If you behave yourself, and weather permitting, we'll try and come up again to see you.'

And Moth had to be content with that, though it seemed hard that her family should have to miss her debut because they would be watching her cousin instead. Somehow, without even being aware of it, Libby was always spoiling things for her just by being Libby.

But one thing Libby couldn't spoil was the excitement of the tour. The company were doing two weeks at provincial theatres, and Moth's group were appearing the first week. They were to go there by train, stay in a hotel, fit in some lessons, and dance every night.

Moth wondered if other parents insisted on the same elaborate preparations as her great-aunt. She had made a list of everything Moth could possibly need, from knickers, socks, tights and leotards to cardigans, tissues and shampoo.

'I'm only going for a week,' she protested, as yet another item was added to the list. 'Anyone would think I was going to boarding school.'

But Great-Aunt Marion's list was nothing to the upheaval wrought by Mrs Blundell-Smith. Moth was at least already one remove from home, but Tom had never been away from his mother.

'I've written to Miss Wren about Tom's chest,' she confided to Miss Graham when she arrived to pick up Moth. 'And I've explained about Tom's tonic and how important it is that she reminds him to take it every day. One can't be too careful in the winter, and I sometimes think these schools are very cavalier. All that dancing round and getting overheated can so easily lead to catching a cold.'

'I'm sure he'll be all right,' said Great-Aunt Marion, who fussed over different things and regarded small boys as hardy animals.

But all the way to the station Mrs Blundell-Smith kept up a stream of reminders. 'I've packed some anti-congestant in case you get a stuffy nose. I've put in two extra pullovers in case it turns very cold. I've explained to Miss Wren that you mustn't sit around in a draughty theatre in that short-sleeved shirt and you must wrap up when you're not on stage.'

Tom wasn't listening. He had perfected a technique for transporting his mind elsewhere and he was thinking about sharing a room with Ben. He had often wished he had a brother and now he would see what it was like.

Miss Wren was darting along the platform like a sheepdog harrying the flock. She had no time to spare for Tom's mother, who wanted to make sure that he was safely stowed in the right carriage.

'Good-bye, darling,' Mrs Blundell-Smith called, as though she was addressing the whole train. 'Have a lovely time and don't forget to ring me every day and let me know how you're getting on. You know I'll be thinking of you.'

Tom moved out of reach of her kiss and thankfully handed the window over to someone else, but Mrs Blundell-Smith stood there blowing kisses until the train was out of sight.

'Bye-bye smother,' said one girl, raising a giggle.

Tom pretended not to hear and went to look for Ben.

9

On tour

It was a short journey, but long enough for Moth and Nadia to bump their way through the swaying carriages to the buffet.

'Funny how different things taste on a train,' said Nadia, as they stood in the corridor draining tins of Coke and watching fields the colour of worn corduroy gallop past. A pale sun flooded flat fields and an occasional church tower disturbed the skyline.

'I've always wanted to have a proper meal on a train,' said Moth, 'I like the idea of doing two things at once. Eating and travelling,' she explained, as Nadia looked puzzled. She had dark, intense eyes under strong eyebrows, and a quiet self-confidence that attracted Moth, who was glad they were going to share a room. Nadia had been in the production the year before.

'We stayed in a super hotel. My room had its own bathroom and a colour TV and an electric coffee-maker. It was such a pity we had to be at the theatre every night, as I was longing to lie in bed and watch TV. Miss Wren says the company always looks after us well and makes sure we stay somewhere nice.'

This year's 'somewhere nice' was in the centre of town, opposite the cathedral, in a street with the curious name of Tombland. 'There are a lot of strange names here,' said Miss Wren when someone made an uneasy joke about the name, 'as you'll see when we go to the theatre. It's a very historic city.'

Moth felt she couldn't be bothered with history for the time being. She was caught up in the luxury of their room, which was just as Nadia had forecast, with a primrose bathroom leading off it.

'No excuse for you to look grubby,' said Miss Wren, when she came round to see how everyone was settling in. 'We're going to have an earlyish high tea, and then you can sort out your things for tomorrow and either watch TV or play a quiet game. And I do mean quiet, because the other guests are paying to be in a hotel not a school. And I recommend early bed, because you've got a very tiring week ahead of you.'

And so began the oddest, busiest, most varied week of Moth's life.

There was the fun of meals in the hotel, in the theatre restaurant, in the elegant Assembly House and, most popular of all, in a dimly lit dive where they served hamburgers and french fries against a background of rock music. Miss Wren hated it and prophesied that they'd all have been deaf after another week.

There was the walk across town to and from the theatre, a walk that changed every day. It was a city of churches and narrow alleyways, some still paved with cobblestones. Medieval houses cross-gartered with timber leaned against neat Georgian shops, and Moth noticed a pink cottage that might have been made of coconut ice. It was, disappointingly, a bank.

And there was the theatre which, alas, was not old. There had been a theatre on the site for over two hundred years, but a previous one had burnt down and been rebuilt in the style of a cinema. Its plain chocolate brown interior lacked the gilding and carved goddesses essential to a real theatre, and it was so vast that Moth was glad she didn't have to make herself heard.

The backstage certainly had the feel of a real theatre, and they stared up into the flies where the scenery was suspended, to be lowered and raised by the ropes and counter-weights that littered the wings. They saw the dressing rooms for the stars and, further away from the stage, the rooms for the chorus that they would be using. 'They're not so handy so that you have something to aim for,' explained the manager, a genial Irishman who had volunteered to show them round and answer any questions. 'That's the lesson of the theatre. You start at the bottom and aim for the top.'

The huge wicker baskets of props and costumes had arrived and were being unpacked by the wardrobe staff. They passed another dressing room already invaded by dancers. One was darning her pointe shoes while another was bashing them against the wall in an attempt to break down their stiffness. Some, partly dressed, were sorting out their make-up, chatting as they squinted at the mirror while putting on eye-liner and mascara. On stage a couple were trying out a lift, aided by a patient pianist who was running through their sequence yet again. The band room was filling up with players and instruments, a stage hand was rigging up the snow and mist, and now it was time to become children and mice for Act One, as Miss Wren brushed and plaited their hair, checked their make-up, and even sewed on the odd hook until the transformation was complete.

There wasn't time to be frightened because there was so much to do. Moth and Nadia made their entrance through the fireplace in one corner of the stage, which was in semi-darkness. As they leapt through the hole a stage-hand let off a flash and they ran forward in genuine surprise. Behind them was Clara with the nutcracker doll and the Christmas tree now unfolded to a towering height. The music hurried on, and the stage was invaded by warring rats and toy soldiers while the mice scurried away to a corner. It was like jumping off a diving board, the moments on stage being like the flight through the air. Moth wanted to take it slowly, to prolong being on stage, but the music marched relentlessly on and she was back in the wings among the chattering snowflakes who were waiting to come on and finish Act One.

The dress rehearsal and the first performance that same evening were a foretaste of what it was like to do two shows a day. And as though this wasn't enough, in the mornings they were obliged to have lessons as laid down by the regulations governing performances by children. Fortunately Miss Wren didn't take them too seriously and turned teaching into sightseeing.

One morning they walked round the cathedral, which had been built by the Normans. Moth was impressed by the great rounded arches decorated with simple wavy lines. They matched the massive chords swelling from the organ which, to her surprise, was being played by a boy. She stared up at him in his perch above the nave, at the side of a cluster of pipes like ranks of golden trumpets. The sound rushed into the empty air, reminding her of the moment when she had looked back at the expanse of the stage and longed to fill it with her dancing.

Another morning they went round to an old merchant's house that had been turned into a museum. The rooms were furnished in the style of different periods, and Miss Wren left them to wander round by themselves, saying that she wanted them to write a short essay about something that had caught their eye.

Nadia decided that she liked the Victorian night nursery best, though she didn't fancy being imprisoned in the cot, which had forbidding-looking bars. She was fascinated by a square, polished wood box containing a lavatory bowl decorated with blue transfers, but Moth pointed out that it would be difficult to write an essay about it. What would you call it for a start?

Moth thought of describing the toy room, which was peopled by intense, rather spiteful-looking dolls. They had fierce glass eyes and very determined expressions, and one had a trunk of clothes that included a tiny whalebone corset. 'She looks glad she isn't wearing that,' Moth said to Nadia. But the toys, though interesting, were sad, and the dolls' houses looked forlorn, as though the inhabitants were very old and could only afford to lead frayed lives.

The house itself was full of odd corners and sloping ceilings, and the wooden floors, slippery with centuries of polish, creaked mournfully. Moth eventually found her subject in the cellar, which contained a collection of old signs that had once hung outside inns and shops to advertise the owner's wares. There was a huge padlock and key for the ironmonger, a faded gilt teapot for the grocer, three golden balls for the pawnbroker, and a cheerful striped pole for the barber. There was also a sinister Chinaman who had once stood outside a tea blenders, but Moth's favourite was a large golden sheep doing his best to look dignified while suspended by a chain round his middle. He was the sign of the Golden Fleece outfitters, and she felt she would have stopped outside their shop often to console him.

There was a matinée on Wednesday, and Thursday found them so exhausted that Miss Wren suggested everyone should wash their hair, write their essay, have an early lunch and then lie down.

Nadia and Moth lay on their beds and for once they were too tired to talk. Nadia felt hot and irritable. She tested her forehead anxiously and wondered whether she had a temperature. She didn't want to ask Miss Wren because she was bound to fuss and perhaps make her stay in bed. I'm not ill, I'm not ill she told herself fiercely, but the theatre seemed far away, such a long, long walk . . .

Moth wasn't looking forward to the performance either. It was exciting, certainly, but she was beginning to feel bruised and battered. First they had to do a warm-up class, then she changed into her mouse skin with its collar and skirt of tweed fur and heavy helmet-like head. Then they crowded into the twilight of the wings, where they were jostled by the corps de ballet. Moth had several times been pushed aside by an impatient soloist, and the prince was anything but princely if one got in his way. Then she had to change into her mermaid's tunic and pin on scratchy tresses made of raffia. This was followed by an even quicker change. There wasn't time to go back to the dressing room: Miss Wren waited in the wings and deftly skinned them as they came off, transforming them into the children who lived in a shoe. Even the moments on stage were not quite as she had imagined: her pulse beat faster, it was a test of quick wits, she was whirled on and off by the music.

'Was it like this last year?' she said, wondering whether Nadia too found the performances an ordeal, but Nadia was asleep.

On one of their routes to the theatre Miss Wren had pointed out a small shop that had been restored to its 18th-century past. The window looked as though it had been ruled into neat squares, and peering through the panes Moth had noticed a packet of Mustard Bath preparation. 'You'll probably all be glad of that by the end of the week,' said Miss Wren, when Nadia scoffed at the idea of smelling of mustard. 'It's a good old-fashioned remedy for aches and pains.' Moth thought of her great-aunt. It would make an unusual and useful Christmas present, but alas the shop was shut.

Now, tired but not tired enough to sleep, this seemed the moment to go back to the shop. There was plenty of time before they had to leave for the theatre and no one would miss her. Nadia stirred uneasily while Moth was looking for her shoes and raincoat, but she didn't wake up.

Moth tiptoed along the corridor and down the stairs. For once the foyer was empty and there was no one behind the reception desk. Outside, a mist like a soft shawl drew the narrow streets together. It wasn't far to the shop, but by the time she arrived the street lights were on and the window glowed as though stoked by fires of mustard. With its cherry red wallpaper, small counter, and shelves of jars, it looked like the set of an 18th-century comedy. She half expected the assistant to be wearing a frock coat and breeches, but he had not been restored and was such a keen modern salesman that she bought not only the mustard bath but an apron for her mother and a yellow notepad for Toby's Christmas stocking.

It put her in the mood for shopping and the windows further up the alley dragged her into their pools of light. Moth let herself be led on. She was too shy to go inside the shops in case she felt obliged to buy something, but she stood for a long time outside a dusty little jewellers, examining the rings and brooches that lay tumbled together.

Bells chimed but she heard them only as the voices of the church towers that stood like sentinels on every

93

corner. Then by chance she saw a clock in one of the shop windows. Its impersonal modern face left no doubt about the time: it was the time at which they were due to leave for the theatre. Moth realised that she had been bewitched and was now late and lost.

She tried at first to make her way back to the hotel. It was opposite the cathedral, and the cathedral was . . . where? It had withdrawn into its close, its direction obscured by darkness so that she felt as though she had been blindfolded and spun round. She sensed the castle high up on its mound, but couldn't tell whether she was going towards or away from it.

She ran down what looked like a familiar street only to find herself in a blind courtyard. The houses round it leant on each other as though they were laughing at her bewilderment. They were secretive, decaying, deceitful. The churches kept their comfort locked within; they needed to defend themselves.

Moth realised that by now the others would have left the hotel, so she began to look for the theatre. I must ask someone the way, she thought desperately, but the streets had emptied. The only people she could see were inside, moving like shadows in the flickering gloom of the television.

At last she reached a central street that was kept alive by a one-way traffic scheme. Neither a youth in a leather jacket nor a man hurrying to the pub had ever heard of the theatre. One woman had been to a show there, but she had gone in the car and wasn't sure of the way. The theatre, Moth discovered, was on the fringe of most people's lives. And then suddenly, as though tired of the game, the streets fell into place and there was the theatre. She raced towards it, round to the stage door and up the stairs to the dressing room. It was empty. Clothes and make-up were scattered about, but there was no sign of the children in their party frocks nor of the mice.

Moth hurried to change, but her costume too had disappeared and she wondered who was inside it. Had Miss Wren produced another mouse out of thin air? She ran back down the stairs and into the wings, her eyes baffled by the half-light. A hand seized her and began to strip off her clothes. She was too dazed to speak or resist, and Miss Wren said nothing. She turned Moth into a mouse in seconds, thrust her headpiece on and pushed her in front of the others, next to Nadia. There was a flash and they were on.

Later that night, when they were getting ready for bed, Nadia told her what had happened.

'Miss Wren was very cool, though I'm sure she was scared that something awful had happened to you. She shut Julia up when she suggested you'd been kidnapped or run over, and she said that if you didn't turn up I'd have to go on by myself and pretend there was only meant to be one mouse. I'm jolly glad you turned up when you did.'

'So am I.' Moth was still shaken by the moment when she had felt herself replaced, deleted from the production. It had been worse than Miss Wren's anger when she had explained that she had gone out shopping and got lost.

'Moth,' Nadia spoke from the bathroom where she was cleaning her teeth, 'I'm glad you're back because I want your advice. Something funny's happened.'

'Something else?' Moth felt too exhausted to cope with any more crises.

'Yes, look.' Nadia's pyjama jacket was undone and she presented herself to Moth as she might have done to a doctor. Her face was flushed and worried and her chest was dotted with red spots.

'I feel all hot,' she said, 'and they won't stop itching. I've been wanting to scratch them all evening, and I'm sure Miss Wren would have noticed if she hadn't been so worried about you. What am I going to do?'

10

Quarantine

Maths, geography, French. It was back to all the things Moth disliked most, and she was finding it especially difficult to concentrate on French dictation. All those accents. She could manage the acutes but wasn't sure about the graves, and as for the circumflexes that looked like pointed hats and the cidillas that trickled down like little tears . . .

She sprinkled a few at random and went back to remembering the previous Monday, when they had been getting ready for the dress rehearsal. She was so far away that she didn't notice that Miss Lambert's secretary had appeared and that Mademoiselle Bec had broken off her final reading of '*l'homme qui epouse une femme muette*' and was addressing her: '*Jennifer*' – Mademoiselle Bec couldn't understand why anyone with a nice English name like Jennifer should prefer such an odd nickname as Moth – '*la directrice vous voir immediatement.*'

Moth was startled. What on earth could Miss Lambert want. She tried hastily to think of anything she had left undone, or done that she shouldn't have done, but her conscience was clear, except for her shopping expedition. Could Miss Wren have reported that? She was further alarmed to find Miss Pearson too in the study, and for once looking worried.

'Sit down,' said Miss Lambert briskly, 'I'm sorry to get you out of class, but I wanted to tell you that the girl you shared a room with on tour has got chicken-pox, and we are worried that it may have spread to the rest of the cast.'

Moth breathed a sigh of relief. 'I'm sure I'll be all right because I've already had it.'

Miss Lambert didn't look equally relieved. 'Well, that's a good start, but I'm afraid it's not quite as simple as that. It is possible to have chicken-pox twice, and you may be a little more at risk than the others as you shared a room with Nadia.'

Moth wasn't quite sure what Miss Lambert was leading up to. She couldn't mean . . . 'I feel fine,' she said defensively, beginning to wonder whether she did feel quite as well as she had done yesterday, 'and I haven't got any spots.'

'Oh, it's too soon for that. I've spoken to our school medical adviser who says the incubation period is about a fortnight, so you won't officially be in the clear for the next two weeks.'

Two weeks. Moth tried to picture the calendar. The opening night was on Boxing Day, and that was surely more than two weeks away. 'What do you want me to do?' she asked suspiciously.

'You live with your great-aunt, don't you?' said Miss Lambert, exhibiting that impeccable memory that amazed and flattered parents. 'I shall have a word with her and explain the situation and suggest that if you do show any signs of being unwell, she should keep you at home. Otherwise, we'll keep our fingers crossed. Have you anything to add?' she asked Miss Pearson, who was still looking unhappy.

'Well there won't be any more rehearsals until we see how the others are. The second group are on tour this week, so if you're clear by the end of the following week it won't be too bad. I suppose we must look on the bright side.'

'Now back to class with you,' said Miss Lambert, 'and I wouldn't mention it to the others. We don't want a full-scale chicken-pox scare just before Christmas.'

'Don't you dare ruin my Christmas show,' implored Miss Pearson, and she flew away, leaving Moth to wander back to the classroom where at least dictation was over.

'What did she want?' said everyone.

'It's a secret,' said Moth, enjoying herself, 'Miss Lambert asked me specially not to tell anyone.'

But no one believed her. After entreating her to tell all, they finally left her alone resentfully. The general feeling was that Moth Graham had become too big for her precious ballet shoes.

Miss Lambert was not the first to tell Great-Aunt Marion. Mrs Blundell-Smith had already been on the line with the bad news.

'I knew something like this would happen,' she said triumphantly, 'some parents are so irresponsible. Fancy letting the child go on tour when she was so obviously sickening. But then some parents will do anything to get their children on the stage, won't they?'

Great-Aunt Marion was glad Mrs Blundell-Smith couldn't see her expression. She privately thought that Mrs Blundell-Smith was just such a parent. 'Well, it's not such a terrible illness,' she said. 'Let's hope that no one else catches it. I gather Moth has already had it once, so she should be all right.'

'Tom hasn't had it,' said Mrs Blundell-Smith, as though infectious diseases were something to be ashamed of, 'and I intend to make sure that he doesn't get it, though I'm afraid it may be a case of locking the stable door. He's staying at home until the incubation period is over, and I shall be keeping a close watch on him. I'm not a mother to sacrifice her child's health, and I shan't allow him to appear unless the whole cast has a clean bill of health.'

'She'll probably insist on inspecting us all to make sure we're not hiding any spots,' said Moth, when her great-aunt told her. 'Poor Tom. Diane calls her his "smother", which is just about right.'

'I expect it's because he's an only child,' said Great-Aunt Marion. 'If Mrs Blundell-Smith had any others to worry about, she probably wouldn't make such a fuss of him. But he seems a nice boy in spite of her. It's such a pity when anyone's life is wrecked by impossible parents, and it happens all too often.'

'It's awful how important parents are,' Moth said reflectively. 'Jane's terribly worried because she's growing so tall, and that's probably because her father is well over six foot. I wonder what affect mine are having on me? Talents like dancing run in families, don't they, but everyone in our family seems so down-to-earth and not in the least artistic.'

'I doubt if it would make all that difference if your parents were both dancers, because famous people hardly ever seem to have children as gifted as they are. Although the Grahams haven't produced any dancers so far, they have shown a pioneering spirit and plenty of determination. I think a lot of vital qualities have come together in you and Libby and suddenly, perhaps, the

100

mixture is right for a dancer. By the way, I shouldn't mention chicken-pox to Libby. She may not have had it, but if she knows about you she may start worrying, and worry pulls you down quicker than anything.'

'I'm the one that worries,' said Moth, 'not her. You don't think I will get it, do you?'

'Most unlikely,' said Great-Aunt Marion firmly. 'But it's all in the hands of fate, and if you're fated to dance, which I'm sure you are, then you'll be all right.'

Moth was unconvinced. Wasn't fate the same as Robert's wheel of fortune, which was moving slowly all the time, taking you up out of the depths but just as surely when you reached the summit winding you down again?

Remembering his words had brought Robert back into Moth's mind and, as so often happens, he materialised the very next day.

Moth saw him wandering along apparently lost in thought, and he would have drifted past without noticing her if she hadn't tugged at the end of his scarf.

'Hi! Penny for your thoughts.'

'They're not worth it,' said Robert mournfully. 'I was wondering whether I shouldn't chuck in my research and get a job like everyone else.'

'Why? Has something awful happened?'

'It is awful in a way, but it isn't what most people call growing up when they really mean growing old. I haven't developed a sudden craving for the security of a nest and a pile of possessions. It's more life-giving than that.'

'Well,' said Moth impatiently, 'what is it?'

Robert looked at her with the same expression of wonderment she had seen on Toby's face when he'd been given a bicycle. 'I've fallen in love,' he said shyly, 'with a girl I met at a party.'

101

'Oh, is that all?' Moth was disappointed. 'And now you want to settle down,' she said flatly, surprised to find how much she hated the thought of the girl and a settled-down Robert.

'Never! But she's a marvellous, beautiful, desirable girl and everyone else is after her. How can I possibly compete without any money?'

'You could try falling in love with someone who doesn't want money spent on her,' said Moth in a practical voice that sounded suspiciously like her mother's. 'If she fancies you she won't care how much money you've got.'

'But I don't want the kind of girl who doesn't mind whether I have any money,' said Robert irritably. 'I want a goddess not a saint, and she's got raven hair and enormous eyes and is as inaccessible as a fairy princess. And that ought to appeal to you. It's your line of country.'

Robert leapt up to touch a branch high above him. He didn't jump like a dancer but he conveyed the same sense of joy.

'Do you mean she's a dancer?'

'Learning to be. I didn't get much chance to talk to her, but I gather she's just gone to the Upper School of the Royal Ballet and she's already deputising for the corps. So if someone suddenly falls ill, she could find herself on stage at Covent Garden.'

'Perhaps someone'll get chicken-pox,' said Moth, thinking of the fate that hung over her. One person's disappointment was always someone else's chance.

'Why on earth should they get that?' said Robert. 'That's a kids' disease,' and then he yelled for mercy as Moth pulled his scarf tighter and tighter.

'Sorry,' he gulped, when she had let go and explained. 'Well, it looks as though I'm in quarantine for love and you're in quarantine for chicken-pox, so perhaps we should try and cheer each other up. I'm planning to queue for the ballet next Tuesday. It's a triple bill programme, so it shouldn't be too popular, and I could probably get you a ticket if you'd like to come. I'm afraid you'd have to pay for yourself,' he added quickly, 'as I'm broke.'

'Yes, please,' said Moth, and then remembering her recent promise, 'providing my great-aunt agrees.'

She did agree, because she trusted Robert and thought that an outing would do Moth good. Although she hadn't said any more about being ill, she suspected that she was fretting over it because she was by temperament what Great-Aunt Marion called a 'worry-mutton'.

The seats were in the back row – more a perch than a seat as Robert put it – so it was as well that he was armed with powerful binoculars. The programme began with *La Bayadère*, which Moth had never heard of but which Robert assured her was one of the highlights of Russian classical ballet and 'literally out of this world'.

She saw the point of this when she read her programme and learnt that only a part of the ballet was still performed and the act they were going to see took place in the Kingdom of the Shades. This was a dreamlike afterlife that the warrior Solor visited in search of his beloved, Nikiya, a temple dancer (a Bayadère) who had been killed by a snake sent by her rival, who planned to marry Solor.

'It's the opening that's so marvellous,' Robert told her. 'Once you've seen the corps de ballet come on, you never forget it. It's one of the most magical entrances ever devised.'

And as the procession of shades began to unfold, Moth saw what he meant.

They came on one at a time, moving along a ramp that sloped gently down to the stage. They were seen in profile, and they advanced slowly, tilting forward into an arabesque at each step. As the first dancers reached the ground they began to form into a line, still repeating the same arabesque movement. And as each continued her unearthly progress down the slope, yet another dancer appeared in her place at the top. Moth felt the back of her neck tingling. So this was how your hair stood on end. The line of dancers now extended into two rows across the stage, each figure obeying an invisible command that stretched it into grave beauty. And still they went on descending. Each time a new dancer appeared Moth felt that there couldn't be any more, and yet there were, so that the Kingdom of Shades seemed truly an eternity.

Robert was scanning the dancers through his binoculars. Suddenly he pushed them into Moth's hand and whispered, 'It's her. The third one from the top.' Moth was reluctant to break the spell but this wasn't a moment to argue. She focused on the ramp and the glasses shot her forward so that she seemed to be only a few inches away from the girl. She could see the details of her make-up, the dark lines emphasising her enormous eyes, her neat black hair, the stiff gauze of her white dress. There was something disturbingly familiar about her. Moth felt that she recognised her, and yet who could it be?

The ballet sped past, with the corps echoing the movements of the soloists or providing a background for their dazzling displays. Solor whirled round the stage, striving to recapture a being who would now always elude him. He tried to bind Nikiya to him with a long filmy scarf that was as ineffective as a mist. It tied the lovers together, and yet because he was alive while she was now a shade their parting was inevitable.

The audience gave a tremendous reception to Solor

and Nikiya, but Moth and Robert saved their greatest applause for the corps de ballet. Robert was so buoyant that Moth half-expected him to soar across the amphitheatre and float down on to the stage.

'Wasn't Marina wonderful!' he said, when the audience finally let go of the soloists.

'Marina!' squeaked Moth. Of course, that was why she looked familiar. They went into the bar to stretch their legs, and there, competing with the jostling chatter and clinking glasses, she told Robert how Marina had been the star pupil of the Fortune School and how she had actually appeared on the same stage with her at the end of term show.

'I used to mind her things,' she said, remembering how willing she had been to wait on the imperious Marina.

'You know her.' Robert was impressed. 'Well, we must go backstage afterwards so that you can congratulate her.'

Moth looked doubtful. She wondered whether the haughty Marina – and it was difficult to reconcile her impression of Marina with the fragile plaything of Robert's dreams – would really welcome a visit from someone she had regarded as an obedient slave or, as Libby had rather cruelly put it, 'Mary's little lamb'.

But Robert was determined to exploit such an unexpected opportunity, and Moth sat through the rest of the evening with a feeling of apprehension. Even Anthony Dowell, who was dancing the part of the young tutor Beliaev in *A Month in the Country*, wasn't able to make her forget the embarrassment that she feared might lie ahead.

It was another ballet about love, this time about the havoc wrought by a handsome student who arrives to tutor the son of a well-to-do Russian family and upsets all the women from the maid to the mistress of the house. Love, as portrayed here, was a teasing, passionate, disturbing affair that turned everything upside down, and Moth realised how potent a force it was. She saw it on the stage, sensed it in Robert beside her, and saw it lying in wait for her in the future. A strange, beautiful, irresistible experience that would one day have to be explored. It was bound up with the world she wanted to inhabit – most ballets seemed to be about love in one form or another – but she was relieved that for the moment she wasn't in love, because she foresaw that when it did happen it would overthrow everything.

She was glad that the final ballet, *Elite Syncopations*, was sheer fun. It had brilliant zany costumes and bounced along to cheerful ragtime music. The audience loved it.

'They don't like being made to feel too much,' muttered Robert darkly, but for once Moth was not on his side. Feeling was so exhausting.

'Come on, let's go.' Robert trod impatiently on several unfeeling feet and took the stairs with the speed of a waterfall, leaving Moth to clatter behind in his wake. People had already clustered round the Stage Door, but Robert pushed past them and walked boldly in.

'Yes?' said a man who was obviously used to quelling the enthusiasm of admirers.

'We've come to see Marina Guest,' said Robert, implying that Marina was expecting them.

'Never heard of her,' said the doorman, blocking their way. 'Try again.'

'She's in the corps de ballet and she's only just joined.'

'The Bayadère lot,' said the man, unimpressed. 'They've gone home, went hours ago. You should have come round in the first interval if you wanted to see them. They don't hang about.'

Saved, thought Moth thankfully, though she could see that Robert was deflated. He resisted all her efforts to make conversation on the way home, and lapsed into a moody silence. He wouldn't come in, even for a coffee, but wandered on without saying good-bye.

Moth felt helpless and discarded. She had been looking forward to the evening so much, and now it had all gone wrong. Robert was unhappy, too unhappy to care whether he spoiled things for someone else. And I'm like that too, she thought, I don't think about other people when I'm unhappy either.

II

Open a new window

Both Moth and Libby had been excused from taking part in the school Christmas Show, but they were expected to attend and were given the job of acting as ushers.

Moth remembered how exciting it had been the previous year when she had appeared as a holly berry. Now the little stage of the studio looked insignificant compared to a real theatre, and yet when she came across the first years getting changed and made up for their Scottish dance, she felt sad at the thought of how irrevocably she had moved on.

The show was designed to impress parents with the wide scope of the newly combined schools. The programme included a lively Scottish reel, a Chopin waltz danced in a simple classical style, a dramatic fencing duel by two boys dressed as Hamlet and Laertes, and a chorus girl number, complete with top hats, long cigarette-holders and fishnet stockings, that made a visible impact on all the fathers in the audience.

But, surprisingly, the success of the evening was scored not by any of the dancers but by Ruth, who came on by herself and told the audience a story. It was a real winter's tale, a cold, shivery, frightening story, and with no more than one or two props – a ball, a scarf, a lantern – Ruth transformed herself into a small boy, an anxious mother, an old gipsy woman. She conjured up scenery and weather and commanded such a rapt silence that it was as though the audience were forgetting to breathe.

Moth was caught up in her spell and stared disbelievingly at the terrifying old woman. Was this really the friend she had once walked home with every day and forfeited over a stupid quarrel about tap shoes?

Ruth's parents were sitting next to Great-Aunt Marion, and Moth and Libby joined them in the interval.

'Wasn't Ruth marvellous?' said Moth, trying to sound as enthusiastic as she felt. She would like to have said something more original, but she felt shy and confused at the sight of Daniel, who looked at her as though he had never seen her before.

'A real *tour de force*,' said Great-Aunt Marion. 'You must be very proud.'

Mrs Fisher beamed. She was an older version of Ruth, dark, short and plump, with blue eyes that outshone her plentiful jewellery. She was wearing a fur coat that, far from looking elegant, suggested some forest creature snug in its winter camouflage.

'Thank you,' she said, 'but your own brood aren't doing too badly either. We're looking forward to seeing Moth in *The Nutcracker*, and we're also going to see Libby's pantomime. Which reminds me,' she sparkled in Moth's direction, 'would you like to come too? I expect you've already made plans to see Libby, but if not, I'm sure Ruth would love you to come with us.'

So Ruth hadn't told her mother about the quarrel. Moth wondered whether she had told Daniel, and hoped not. She badly wanted to make it up, but was this the right way? Wouldn't Ruth be annoyed that her mother had interfered, and furious with Moth for accepting the invitation? Everyone was waiting for her to reply, and she found herself admitting that she hadn't made any arrangements yet and that, yes, she would love to go with the Fishers.

'Good. We're going on Friday and we'll pick you up about six,' said Mrs Fisher as she turned away to be congratulated again on having such a talented daughter.

The rest of the week saw the start of the holidays and the virtual disappearance of Libby, whose life was now divided between evening rehearsals and mornings in bed. The rehearsals, they gathered, were long and exhausting, and culminated in a dress rehearsal at which so many things went wrong that it seemed impossible that the show was about to open. Tempers were short, there were endless waits while some miraculous stage effect was perfected, the wings had become death-traps of ropes, counterweights and scenery, and there were sixty-nine steps from the stage to the dressing rooms.

And yet, a tired Libby told them when she finally arrived home after the first night, it was worth it all because the audience made all the difference.

'You remember the boy you spoke to,' she said to Moth. 'Well there's a moment when he tells his partner in crime that they're on their own and there's nobody else there. The little man doesn't believe him and says to the audience "Y're not there". "Oh yes we are", they shout back, and they are very much there. All the time I was on stage I could feel them, not like a conventional sea of faces, but as though they were a dangerous wild animal. You couldn't tell what it might get up to next.'

Moth thought Libby was exaggerating, but she had

forgotten, until she herself became part of it, that a pantomime audience is indeed a very special beast.

There was no chance to say anything in private to Ruth in the car. Mrs Fisher flashed Moth a welcome but Ruth said nothing, and Moth's place on the back seat was next to an aloof Daniel, who made it plain that he was only coming along to humour his parents.

It's up to me to make the first move, Moth told herself, conscious of Daniel beside her in the darkness and wishing he didn't make her feel so nervous.

'I loved your piece at the Christmas show,' she said, lobbing the words across Daniel to Ruth, 'I had no idea you were such a good actress. You're never like that in class.'

She wondered if Ruth had heard her, but Dr Fisher, who was driving, said, 'I always thought my uncle's talent would turn up somewhere in the family. He was a very promising actor, and I think Ruth may take after him.'

'Is he famous?' said Moth, hoping he wasn't someone she ought to have heard of.

'He's dead,' said Dr Fisher sadly. 'He died during the war, before he had a chance to become more than a very promising student. But I think the Fishers are more likely to turn out an actress than a dancer. We're the wrong shape for that, aren't we, my dear?' And he glanced affectionately at his wife.

'Yes, I'm afraid so. It does seem hard that these things are decided by forces beyond our control. We were all so disappointed when Miss Lambert said she wouldn't advise Ruth to go on with ballet as a career, but perhaps it was for the best. It's made you concentrate much more on drama, hasn't it?'

So Ruth had given up ballet because she wasn't the

111

right build for a dancer. Moth remembered that her great-aunt had suggested that this might be the reason, but she had brushed it aside because she didn't want to admit that the quarrel had been her fault. But why on earth hadn't Ruth explained? Because she didn't want to tell people that she was getting too fat, and perhaps also because she had dearly wanted to be a dancer, and Moth's relentless ambition had rubbed salt in the wound. We shall never be real friends again, thought Moth sadly. If I had to give up dancing, I wouldn't want to know someone who went on about it all the time and still had a chance of making it.

The foyer of the theatre was swarming with small children in charge of indulgent parents. The 'buy me something' racket was in full swing, and every child was armed with something: a packet of crisps, a tube of sweets, a funny mask. Some of the children were too small to cope with the seats and stood in wonderment between the rows, waiting impatiently for this new unknown treat.

'I'd hate to have to perform before that lot,' said Daniel, making it quite clear that he wasn't part of the audience. 'I bet they won't stop talking or eating.'

'Wait till they get caught up in audience participation,' said Dr Fisher, who was obviously prepared to enjoy himself. 'That's what pantomimes are all about.'

And he was right. The rehearsal Moth had seen was the roughest sketch for the finished production and she marvelled at the transformation. Scenes and characters were coloured in, the Peri popped out of the bottle with a silver flash, Mrs Sinbad, who arrived on stage on roller skates and wore the most outrageous wigs, used real ingredients to make her pastry – and then threw it at the audience. Moth saw why Libby felt they were unpredictable. Most of them were bored by the love scenes and stirred and wriggled as Sinbad and Princess Yasmin sang of their love, but they hissed the wicked Old Man of the Sea as soon as he set foot (and it was a very large, gouty foot) on the stage and picked up every cue aimed at them, shouting advice at any character who asked for it.

As in all pantomimes, there was the traditional song for everyone to join in. All those on the left competed lustily with all those on the right, and then came a bold innovation: Mrs Sinbad and her nephew Tinbad invited all the children under ten to come up on to the stage.

Some of the children, like a little girl next to her who reminded Moth of her sister Lyn, were reluctant at first, but as the braver ones began to stream down the aisles and crowd up on to the stage, they too joined in.

'It's just like the Pied Piper,' said Dr Fisher, as the children were stacked in eager rows. 'Are you sure you two don't want to join in?'

'We're *not* under ten,' chorused Moth and Ruth indignantly, while Daniel looked amused and superior.

They all want to be on the stage, thought Moth, noticing how some of the children had already begun to project themselves. Several of the girls danced as they sang and would happily have stayed up there for the rest of the evening. They had tasted the thrill of being on stage, felt the glare of the footlights, and they didn't want to go tamely back to their seats.

Libby's enjoyment was equally apparent. She made a lively urchin who teased Sinbad, fluttered gracefully through the glittering ballet that greeted Sinbad's arrival on the Diamond Isle, and shook her spear vigorously as she and her fellow pygmies capered round Sinbad and his mother, who had been captured by a cannibal giant and looked destined for the stew pot. It was just one of a series of exotic adventures that involved sherbet smugglers, pirates, slave girls, good and evil spirits, magic carpets, flying umbrellas, explosions and puffs of smoke, a chase round the theatre and a man-eating centipede. 'Open a new window,' sang the cast, emphasising the importance of adventures, 'open a new door', and Moth felt that she and Libby had done just that this term. Libby's happiness ran into hers like the colours in one of Lyn's paintings, overlapping and staining Christmas and the days ahead with a bold promise of joy. If only we could stay still for a moment, she thought, but already the show was over and Libby was taking her curtain call.

'Not bad for a kids' show,' conceded Daniel as they were swept along by the tide of children clamouring for camel masks and cackling like the Old Man of the Sea. In their wake they left the theatre littered like a Bank Holiday beach.

'I suppose they enjoyed themselves,' said Dr Fisher, looking disapprovingly at the discarded cartons and sweet papers, 'but I wish public enjoyment wasn't such a public mess. What an untidy careless creature man is.'

'I loved it,' said Mrs Fisher, trying to divert her husband from what promised to be the start of a familiar lecture. She looks like a squirrel, thought Moth, as Mrs Fisher darted ahead and then looked back, inviting the others to follow her.

'We've got to go round to the stage door and pick up Libby. I said we'd give her a lift home.'

The air outside feathered their faces with cold. It was snowing, and cars and buildings had changed their shapes and teased them with blankness. It was hard to find the stage door in the slippery darkness.

Several of the cast passed them as they toiled up the infamous sixty-nine steps. Moth recognised them but saw she was a stranger to them. This time next week, she thought, I shall be back on the right side of the curtain.

The dressing rooms were strewn with costumes and a

harassed teacher was trying to sort them on to hangers. Daniel seized Libby's grass skirt and waved it tauntingly in front of his hips. Ruth looked longingly at Libby's fuzzy wig; she wanted to try it on. Mrs Fisher unexpectedly produced a box of chocolates and presented them to Libby with an extravagant kiss.

'You were wonderful,' she said, 'and it's a lovely show.'

There was a shy silence as Libby opened the chocolates and handed them round, and then an excited child burst in with a box full of intriguing little parcels. 'It's a present,' she said, 'from Blackbeard to his pygmies.'

There was much scrabbling at tissue paper before the packets disclosed brooches in the shape of butterflies, with bright enamelled wings. Libby pinned hers on at once. She was almost too tired to get dressed – 'It's my ninth change today' – but when she saw the snow she rushed to throw a snowball at Daniel. 'I've never seen it before,' she explained, as Daniel brushed furiously at his neck, 'it never snows at home.'

Moth longed to pelt Daniel with snowballs too. Serve him right, she thought, he's so cool and distant. Why can't he be friendly and try to like us?

They drove home along roads muffled with snow. It lay along the branches of the trees and clung to the bushes in wind-blown patterns.

'It won't last,' said Mrs Fisher sadly, 'but it looks so beautiful now. It's the proper ending for a pantomime and the right prelude to Christmas.'

Libby had fallen asleep, lulled by the purring warmth, and her head drooped against Moth's shoulder. On Moth's other side brother and sister sat as silent as the snow. She wondered if they too were asleep, but when a passing car lit up Daniel's face she saw his eyes shining. It struck her at that moment that she also disliked him because he was so handsome. There was something disturbing about his dark hair and full lips, though she wasn't sure why, and she turned to look instead down the white tunnel opened up by the brilliance of the headlights.

12

In the wings

Mrs Fisher was right. The snow didn't last. The year seemed to stand still. Moth was used to feeling that Christmas would never come, but this year she was waiting even more impatiently for the day after: her first London first night.

She had stopped examining herself for spots, and when the cast gathered for a run-through so that they could get used to a different stage, there turned out to be no further chicken-pox casualties. Mrs Blundell-Smith, however, insisted on staying for the rehearsal and sat in the stalls apparently beaming protective rays around Tom.

The waiting was worse because life with Great-Aunt Marion was so sedate and static. Moth knew now how he felt, the boy in Libby's pantomime who wasn't going home for Christmas. She realised how much she loved her family and how much she missed fighting with Toby and Lyn's perpetual attempts as the youngest to catch up with them. Although when she was home she often longed for some space in which to grow up, she felt a sudden attachment to the small room she shared with Lyn, who would wake up at dawn on Christmas morning, unwrap the most intriguing shapes in her stocking and then wrap them up again because she was supposed to wait for the grand family opening of presents.

Lyn was still at the age when her presents were a complete surprise, whereas Moth was now asked what she would like and sometimes given money. It was a sensible precaution, but the best presents, she thought, were not only just what you wanted but wore a mysterious paper disguise.

She was trying to achieve this on Christmas Eve, when she took herself off to her room to wrap up her presents. Nobody could guess a mustard bath, but it was difficult to impart an air of mystery to Libby's ballet book, which was obstinately book-like. Her most baffling present would undoubtedly be the collection of jokes she had got for Toby. She did each one up separately: the fake chocolate biscuit, the sucker guaranteed to glue cup to saucer, a magic nail that apparently went right through the finger, a horribly realistic spider, and two long pointed fangs as worn by Dracula.

Earlier Moth and Libby had decorated the Christmas tree with the baubles that Great-Aunt Marion had treasured for years. She had preserved them carefully in tissue paper, and their unusual shapes and colours were unlike any modern decorations. Some had strange little grinning faces; there was a scarlet chubby Father Christmas, a glass bell as fragile as a bubble, a rosy-cheeked fairy with a fan-like skirt of soft feathers, a top streaked with glowing rainbows. Even the tinsel had kept its brightness.

'Some of them are older than your father,' said Great-Aunt Marion, distressed to find one in pieces. 'I expect it seems odd to you that I should have looked after them like this, but they're a part of my Christmas, like memories.'

Libby thought this was sentimental. 'Think of all the time you've spent wrapping things up,' she said, 'and all the boxes of the past you've piled up. They take up more room than the present.'

But Moth was glad that her great-aunt had kept them. She liked the idea that her father had seen them when he was Toby's age.

At home the house would be full of noise: carols on the radio while her mother did last-minute cooking; Toby glued to the TV; Lyn over-excited and in everyone's way; her father looking for his slippers and grumbling about having to turn out on a night not fit for a dog to fetch in more coal. Here all was still, as though they were waiting for the sound of angel voices, but when the summons came it was more mundane: the front-door buzzer. Moth heard Libby run downstairs and then there was a single joyous shriek: 'Daddy!'

'I thought I'd stand in for Father Christmas,' said Rex Graham, when he had disentangled Libby and was greeting Moth and his aunt. 'I take it you didn't warn them that I might be coming, as I don't think this one's that good an actress yet.' He pulled Libby's hair playfully. 'I wasn't sure whether I'd get a duty flight that would fit in, but I managed to pull a few strings and here I am.'

From then on Christmas took off. When Captain Graham was at the controls he liked the crew and the passengers to enjoy themselves. On Christmas morning he and Libby and Moth went out for a bracing walk, striding along streets that were deserted except for the occasional child wobbling along on a brand-new bicycle. They came back to an enormous meal that floated on bubbles and hiccups of champagne, and then it was time to open the presents. Great-Aunt Marion gave them identical surprises: a theatrical make-up box each.

They were made of black enamelled tin. There was a mirror in the lid and a tray that lifted off to reveal more compartments underneath that were stacked with sticks and tubes of greasepaint. They were labelled light tan, brownish tan, ivory, sallow pink, brick red, black, deep brown, white, carmine, light blue, and green. There was also powder, putty for making false noses, crêpe hair and spirit gum, false eyelashes, various brushes, cleansing cream, and even some stuff for blacking out teeth and a small bottle of stage blood.

'I shall know where to come if ever I need a disguise,' said Uncle Rex admiringly as Moth and Libby marvelled over the contents, longing for an excuse to use them. His presents were even more extravagant, though, as he explained with a wink, they had involved a little unofficial smuggling. They were cassette radios, with a pre-recorded tape each and a couple of blanks so that they could make their own recordings. Moth's cassette read: Tchaikovsky, *The Nutcracker*, Ballet in Two Acts, Op. 71.

'How did you know? Did Libby tell you?'

'No, and I can't claim any of the credit. I asked the girl in the store for something suitable for a couple of young ballet enthusiasts, and that's what she came up with. I'm glad it's such a success.'

Moth couldn't wait to try it. She slipped the cassette in place and the Overture marched out into the room. It was the curtain going-up-music, and the last time she had heard it, it had been relayed over the tannoy into the dressing room. She knew it by now as she had never known any piece of music before.

'I'm afraid I've let you in for a lot of that,' said Uncle Rex apologetically, but Great-Aunt Marion had had too much champagne to mind.

The champagne lasted into an evening of wild and silly games. They played Happy Families, though as Libby pointed out most of the families didn't look very happy, and mimed titles, though no one seemed to have seen the same films or read the same books. Even snakes and ladders, Great-Aunt Marion's favourite, was more fun with Uncle Rex, who rattled the dice like a real gambling man. They drank to the success of *Sinbad the Sailor,* they drank to the success of *The Nutcracker,* and finally, at Moth's suggestion, they toasted all those who had to be away from home at Christmas.

Just before she fell asleep that night, Moth reached out for her cassette radio and turned it on very softly. She could hear the music more clearly in the dark, and she let it play until it came to her entrance.

The rest of the family arrived after lunch on Boxing Day, bringing the familiar bedlam with them. 'Though I can't think why two more children should make such a difference,' remarked Great-Aunt Marion, for once driven to raising her voice.

There were more presents to unwrap, revealing books on ballet, records, a housecoat for Libby, swansdown slippers and a folding umbrella for Moth and, from her parents, a red leather jewel box.

'I'm sorry we can't afford to stock it with jewels,' said her father, who felt outclassed by the cassette radios, 'but as you're always losing the few jewels you have got and accusing other people of taking them, we thought they ought to have a proper home.'

Toby was delighted with the jokes but refused to let anyone see them. 'I won't be able to use them,' he explained, 'if you've all seen them first.' Great-Aunt Marion had given him a conjuring set, and he retired to a corner and immersed himself in an introduction to magic. Lyn was less easy to silence. She wanted to sit on Uncle Rex's knee and be made a fuss of, and he was forced to tickle her and tip her upside down at regular intervals.

They were all having tea when the Blundell-Smiths arrived. Tom was carrying a present for Moth which his mother insisted he gave her nicely.

'Don't just push it at her, darling,' she cooed, 'that's not the way for a gentleman to give a present to a lady.'

Tom went red and muttered 'Hope you have a happy Christmas,' while Moth, equally embarrassed, gave him her present.

She undid the gift under the watchful eye of Mrs Blundell-Smith, who was obviously anticipating her joy, and was dismayed to find that it was another folding umbrella. She hoped the one from her aunt June was out of sight. Mrs Blundell-Smith started to say that she hoped Moth would appreciate the soft colours, which were so feminine and had been chosen by Tom himself, when she was interrupted by Toby.

'I'm sorry,' he said in a suspiciously polite voice, 'but I thought you'd like to know that there's a huge spider crawling across your lap.'

Mrs Blundell-Smith's scream of terror was deeply satisfying. Even the instructions hadn't predicted anything quite so extreme. Mrs Blundell-Smith had leapt up and was imploring her husband to take the dreadful thing away. Moth saw that Tom was delighted. It more than made up for the folding umbrella. But she was furious with Toby: she was going to need Mrs Blundell-Smith and her car a lot over the next three weeks.

The situation was saved by Uncle Rex. Years of coping with hysterical passengers had developed a gift for sympathy and tact, and he calmed and comforted

Mrs Blundell-Smith while discreetly dosing her with Great-Aunt Marion's whisky.

It was now time for them to leave for their respective theatres. Great-Aunt Marion, Uncle Rex, the Grahams, Libby, Toby and Lyn folded themselves into one car, while Moth and Tom shared the vast back seat of the Blundell-Smith limousine. 'I hope they arrive safely,' said Mrs Blundell-Smith, casting a disapproving and pitying glance at the Grahams' much smaller car. Mr Blundell-Smith said nothing. He seldom spoke.

They cruised smoothly across London, down to the river and over Waterloo Bridge. The familiar landmarks hung in the dusk: St Paul's on the left, Big Ben on the right, both lit with a soft golden glow. The car turned right and purred past concrete towers. The Festival Hall, dressed overall with lights, was moored on the river.

'We know the way, we know the way,' shouted Moth and Tom, dragging their bags out of the car and running towards the Stage Door before Mrs Blundell-Smith could catch up with them.

The atmosphere in the dressing room was as lively as the first day of term. Some of the others had already arrived and were helping Miss Wren unpack the costumes.

'Hullo. Happy Christmas. Get changed quickly. We're going to do a short class first.'

Next door Moth could see and hear the girls of the corps changing. Dancers went up and down the corridor, calling to each other. As they trouped off for their class Moth peeped into the auditorium. The stage hands were still arranging the set and tonight's stars, devoid of glamour, were practising a lift. A boy balancing a tray of sandwiches for the bar pushed past her, and an elderly programme-seller in decorous black settled down to rest her feet and watch the class.

Pliés. Stretching exercises. Up, back, recover, tendu. Miss Wren demonstrated the movement and then counted the beats. 'Some of you seem to have had too much Christmas dinner.' She drilled them relentlessly, forcing the suppleness back into limbs that had only taken a few days off. Moth saw why professionals kept up the daily routine of class.

When they got back to the dressing room, a stage hand arrived with a pile of cards and telegrams. 'Good luck to all my nuts' read the one from Miss Wren. Moth found she had three and a half greetings: a card from Libby and Great-Aunt Marion inscribed 'Watch your step'; a telegram that said REACH FOR THE STARS STOP PROUD LOVE STOP MUMMY DADDY TOBY LYN; a scented card covered in roses signed 'Good luck, Belinda' (Belinda!) 'and John Blundell-Smith'; and a card that she shared with Tom from Miss Pearson and all at the Fortune School.

Soon the floor was littered with envelopes as all the mirrors were festooned with cards. There were cries of 'Who's yours from?' and laughter at some of the witty messages which included a lot of jokes about Chinamen. Julia had been sent a huge box of chocolates that she started to hand round, but Miss Wren looked doubtful. 'Dance first and stuff afterwards' was her advice.

Over the tannoy they could hear the first guests arriving at the Stahlbaums' party, and Moth pictured Tom running round the stage with his toy engine.

'All right mice, your turn now.' Miss Wren led them into the wings and positioned the first two mice behind the fireplace. Nearby crouched a stage hand waiting to touch off the flash and the cloud of smoke.

'Good luck.' There was a crash from the orchestra, the flash went off, and Moth jumped through the hole. At last she had made her London début.

13

Stage-struck

The moments Moth enjoyed most during the next three weeks were those she spent in the wings. Officially she was not supposed to be there, except when she was waiting to go on, because there was very little room and it was a dangerous place, a tangle of ropes, scaffolding and chunks of scenery. The stage had been built to house an orchestra, not a theatre company, and so there was no space up above in which to fly the scenery. Everything had to be pushed on and off, and the scene-shifters manhandled the furniture at such speed that it skated across the stage, arriving in the wings with the force of a battering ram.

They were supposed to wait in the dressing room or in a room that had been rigged up with a television screen that showed what was happening on the stage. But the flat, foggy picture was only a grey shadow of the live performance; what Moth wanted was the backstage thrill of seeing how the illusions worked.

There was the revolving disc that made the snow fall in whirls of light as the guests arrived for the Stahlbaums' party. There were the wires that drew the Christmas tree slowly up to its towering height. There were the two men with carrier bags of snowflakes who climbed on to a catwalk above the stage and dropped their confetti in handfuls over the snowflake ballet. And there was the acrid smell of smoke and spent flashes left by the battle of the rats and the soldiers.

Some of the most impressive magic happened while Moth was on stage. Act II opened with the three Stahlbaum children, Louise, Clara and Fritz, voyaging in a dream-boat across the Lemonade Sea to the Kingdom of Sweets. While their boat floated across the stage – pedalled by a stagehand who sat out of sight in the hull – Moth and the other mermaids combed their tresses amid swirls of misty foam that was piped on to the stage by a machine that looked like a giant vacuum-cleaner. The mist bounced across the stage like a gentle cloud, but it had the choking fumes of a Dickensian London fog. As one of the corps de ballet remarked sourly, 'I bet it's poison. We all used to cough like mad after a dose of that in *Swan Lake*.' Moth overheard her and knew she would remember this the next time she saw *Swan Lake*. She found it hard to adjust to the matter-of-fact realism of the corps, who seemed to spend most of their time gossiping about boyfriends or complaining about their partners.

One moment they would be chattering away as though they were queuing outside a cinema, and the next they would take off on to the stage like ducklings plopping off the bank and into the water. The transformation from girls into snowflakes or flowers was immediate, but it was reversed as soon as they got back to the dressing room where they started complaining again.

'My God, what were they playing at! Did you hear that boob by the orchestra! Who left that damn branch so far out? That floor's a menace. I've got snowflakes stuck in my hair . . . '

And yet Moth saw that they did care about the performance and were easily upset. She was shocked when one of the snowflakes burst into tears and sobbed piteously because she had made a mistake, a mistake that probably no one in the audience would have noticed. Their emotions, like their balance, were fragile, and were always toppling over or flaring up.

The stars were just as volatile. The Prince, as Karl became in Act II, waited in the wings wearing mackintosh leg-warmers over his exquisite white tights and pawed the ground like an impatient racehorse. Louise, dressed as the Sugar-Plum Fairy, was wrapped in a scarf and woollen leg-warmers and kept practising pliés as though she was winding herself up for the moment when she had to dart on stage. She was one of the changes that had been made to this version of *The Nutcracker*, and she had been added to the story by the choreographer because he wanted Clara and Fritz to have a sister who was old enough to fall in love with the passion suggested by the music of the great adagio. The pas de deux was a partnership between two determined individuals that must look, to the audience, like the effortless consummation of a great love. From the wings Moth could see that it wasn't really this, but also she could see how the illusion existed in those few bright yards where everything a dancer learned and practised was put to the test.

When Miss Wren came to find her, her reproof was softened by the sight of Moth's wondrous involvement in the performance.

'Don't you wish it was you, that it would soon be your turn to go on?' Moth whispered. 'I don't know how you can bear just to watch us do it.'

'Well I did dance at one time. I was in the company for quite a long time.'

'And then what happened? Why did you give up?'

'I hurt my knee and it wouldn't stand up to this kind of pressure.'

'Don't you miss it terribly? I think if I had to give up I'd want to go as far away as possible, so as not to be reminded.'

Miss Wren smiled. 'Believe it or not, I get just as much pleasure out of teaching. It has its own thrills, like when you discover someone who you think has the makings of a great dancer. I also enjoy keeping in touch with the company and having a taste of backstage life again, but I wouldn't want to go back to it full-time. It's a very demanding life and very hard work, which is one reason why it's a good idea for someone of your age to get some practical experience. Now you know what those few minutes on stage and the applause at the end really cost.'

While they were talking, the Prince had been circling the stage in a chain of outstretched leaps. Moth could hear and feel the audience responding, almost as though they were breathing faster, and when he finally alighted and spun to rest, they burst out clapping. Moth could see the sweat running down his neck and his hair clung together in wet points. He ran off gracefully and stood in front of them, grabbing a tissue to mop up the sweat while his body still heaved with exertion. Now it was the Sugar-Plum Fairy's solo, chimed by the celeste, an instrument that Tchaikovsky had immortalised with this one haunting little tune, as brittle as icing. Moth remembered dancing to it and blushed at the memory of how amateur she'd been.

On the days when there was a matinee they would have a picnic in the dressing room in between performances. They sat on the floor and swapped sandwiches, and Moth wore the dragon coat. It stood out among the dressing gowns and demure flowered housecoats and made her look as though she was still in costume, but Moth didn't mind. One of the corps de ballet had asked her where she bought it and had fingered the glowing silk enviously.

After tea they would go upstairs to one of the empty lounges and sit watching the river light up and the evening audience drifting in for an early snack or a rendezvous at the bar. Later came the families with children, usually little girls in long dresses with velvet headbands. Already it was January and soon there was only a week to go, then three days, and then it was the last night.

By now the sets and costumes were more real than the rest of the day. The Stahlbaums' drawing room actually existed, and Moth felt that once she was dressed as a mouse she would only have to find the fireplace and she could jump through it into Clara's dream. It didn't seem possible that it could be dismantled and stored away until next year, when someone else would wear her costume.

Nadia, declared free of spots, had been allowed back for the last few days and she shared Moth's feeling of sadness.

'You don't think we might be here again next year?' said Moth hopefully, reminded that it was Nadia's second year with the company.

'Afraid not. They choose you partly by height. Last year I was the right size for one of the small costumes, but by next year we'll both be far too tall.'

Moth sighed. Growing up had its drawbacks. She tried discussing her feelings with Libby, but she was cheerfully anticipating the end of the pantomime.

'I've had enough of being carted around by other people's parents and running up and down all those

131

stairs. And I'm sick of all those changes. Part of me is more than ready to drop out, and yet if they suggested letting someone else do my part for the last few days, I know I'd hate it. As long as the show goes on, I want to be part of it, and I shall miss the others. We're a real company, but the other dancers don't seem to have much time for you.'

Moth knew what she meant. Libby's loyalty was to the cast, who teased and spoilt the kids, as they thought of them. They had come together for a few weeks' security, and they made an extra effort to be friends because they knew they would soon be returning to the uncertainty of calls from their agents, and a couple of days' filming or an audition for TV. But the dancers were part of a regular company and had no need of outsiders, and so Moth's loyalty was to *The Nutcracker* itself. She felt that she knew every phrase of the music. It lived inside her so that she would hear it in the street or before she fell asleep, and she knew that it had marked her as surely as the progress of a year is marked on the wood of a tree.

They got a special cheer from the audience on the last night, and the principals stepped aside and motioned them forward. They walked down to the footlights and stared out into the audience. Great-Aunt Marion, her mother and father, Toby and Lyn were out there somewhere, but Moth was dazzled and could only see a spangled darkness.

Afterwards they came round to the dressing room and Tom took Toby off to show him the backstage.

The dressing room was noisy and crowded. Everyone's parents seemed to have arrived and they all wanted to congratulate Miss Wren. The air buzzed with compliments. 'Jolly good.' 'You were marvellous.' 'Were you the second one along?' Even Lyn got caught up in the

132

praise. 'What were you?' asked an enthusiastic father who was determined to be nice to everyone. And Lyn, making a start as an actress, said unblushingly, 'A mermaid.'

Moth felt that she loved everyone, even Mrs Blundell-Smith, who was bellowing in her father's ear. Suddenly Tom reappeared and pressed something into her hand. 'It's some snowflakes,' he whispered. 'I found them on the stage and I thought you might like to keep them as a souvenir.' They were hard to hold on to, but Moth managed to squeeze through to her dressing table and tip them into her make-up box.

It was time to change, pack up, go home.

'Don't forget your cards,' called Miss Wren, as dressing tables were emptied and holdalls began to bulge with possessions. Moth ripped hers off the mirror and stuffed them in her bag.

'You've still got your make up on,' said Lyn, but it didn't matter. Moth wanted to get out before she cried. There was nothing to celebrate, and she hardly spoke on the way home.

'I think this one's worn out,' said her father, puzzled by her silence. 'I think she'd better go straight to bed.'

'Wouldn't you like some supper?' said her mother, 'Great-Aunt Marion's prepared one of her special treats.'

Moth shook her head. She wasn't hungry.

'All the more for us, all the more for us,' chanted Toby unfeelingly, but Moth didn't care.

She went upstairs, got undressed and straight into bed. She was asleep before she remembered that she hadn't removed her make up, and the next morning her pillow was smudged with lipstick. It was all that was left of *The Nutcracker*.

14

What Next?

It was cold enough for snow on the first day of the 'spring' term, but the sky was too sullen to oblige. Moth could see patterns of frost lacing the window from her bed, and she was reluctant to leave its seductive warmth. She had been scratchy and irritable the last few days, but now that the holidays were over, she didn't want to plunge back into activity.

'I suppose it's safe to expect you both home at a reasonable time today,' said Great-Aunt Marion over breakfast. 'I don't imagine there'll be any extra classes or secret rehearsals yet.'

It was meant as a joke, but Moth frowned. She hated being reminded that *The Nutcracker* was now no more than a dream, that there was nothing to look forward to but the dreary routine of school.

Libby helped herself to another piece of toast. 'Is there any peanut butter left?' she said.

'I think so, in the cupboard. Go and help yourself. I shall never get used to laying the table for someone who wants peanut butter for breakfast. That's your fourth slice, whereas Moth hasn't even finished her egg.'

'I don't want any more.' Moth pushed the remains of her boiled egg away. The congealing golden yolk made her feel sick.

The feeling of not being hungry, of not wanting to join in, lasted all morning. She was surrounded by chatter and clamour. Bells rang. Classes surged up and down the corridors. Everywhere there was the sound of feet running. Everyone had new plans: a new play, a new set of irregular verbs, a new period in history. The staff seemed to have made a host of New Year resolutions that they were impatient to carry out. There was even a new member of staff, who was young and blonde, wore a gold chain round her ankle, and planned to reorganise the school library.

The most painful, because it was the most physical, tonic was administered by a breezy Miss Pearson.

'Yes, I know it's cold,' she said, looking unsympathetically at the class huddled round a luke-warm radiator, 'but the cure is to start generating a little heat of your own. So let's start with a few breathing exercises. Some of you look as though you haven't been breathing properly since last term. Now I want you to take a really deep breath and stretch right up above your head, as far as you can. Then bring your arms down slowly as you breathe out.'

She nodded at the class pianist, an elderly woman who had taken the precaution of wearing mittens and a fur coat and was thawing her fingers on a mug of coffee. She began to play stretching music that drove the air rhythmically in and out of them.

It was like swimming. The first touch of the water was a shock, a challenge to be resisted; then as it crept slowly up it became a possibility, an actuality, a pleasure. The exercises at the barre and in the centre cajoled and eased the suppleness back into their limbs, helped along by some heavy sarcasm from Miss P. 'Are you really trying to do it?' she asked Moth, 'or just leaving it to faith, hope and charity? Look at yourself in the mirror. You can see what's wrong, can't you?'

Moth could.

They ended up with a few exercises on pointes and then settled down for one of Miss Pearson's regular, start-the-term lectures.

'You're coming along well as a class, and I think you're beginning to recognise your individual problems. This term we shall be working for the next Cecchetti exams and I thought we might also have a go at the Pavlova trophy. It's awarded for the best short ballet devised by a class, and there are marks for imagination and invention as well as for the actual dancing. It means a lot of work, I warn you, which is why I'm asking you first whether you'd like to take part.'

'Yes, yes.' The chorus was unanimous.

'Good. Well I've got some ideas for a sequence, but I want some suggestions from you too. Try and find some music you'd like to dance to, or a story that you think might be suitable. I'm not going to do all the work. It's got to be a real group effort.

'I know one or two of you have had some experience of how choreographers work. Now it's your turn. Start listening to music. Look around and see if there's anything that could be turned into a ballet. It could be something you've read, something that happens to you on the way to school, some feeling or sensation. Even the raw material of dancing itself, such as preparing for a class or waiting in the wings. Right, off you go, and put your thinking caps on.'

Moth was already thinking as she went down to the cloakroom. She felt better. It was good to be back to the routine of class, which wasn't dull even though it

138

always followed the same lines. The only way forward lay in becoming a better dancer, and this, she saw, never came to an end. There was always something new to master, just as in the months ahead they would spend more time on pointe until they could balance well enough to take their fingertips off the barre and stand aloft. And dancing wasn't just about performing. As Miss Pearson had suggested, it was also a way of exploring life, of making new patterns and discoveries.

Suddenly she became aware that Ruth was also getting ready to go home. They had met briefly after a performance of *The Nutcracker*, when Mrs Fisher, generous as ever, had come backstage with her usual box of chocolates. Her warmth and praise, echoed by Ruth, made Moth realise how much she needed friends to share her success. And it couldn't have been easy for Ruth.

Moth tried to think what to say when they found themselves outside at the same moment and began to walk along the street together. Should she tell Ruth about the Pavlova competition and ask her advice? She wanted to find some suitable music, something unusual. Perhaps Ruth would have some ideas.

'What sort of music does Daniel play?' she asked.

Ruth looked surprised. 'I'm not sure,' she said. 'Why?'

Moth told her about Miss P.'s talk and how they were going to create a new ballet. 'I want to help,' she said, 'and I wish I knew something about music, but I don't know where to begin. But Daniel might know. Do you think it would be worth asking him?'

Ruth considered it. 'He plays a lot of French and Russian music,' she said, 'and some of it certainly sounds like ballet music. I suppose you could come round and listen to some. I'll ask Mummy. She's very good at persuading Daniel to be co-operative.'

'Could you?' It was a heartfelt plea, but Moth didn't want to spoil things by saying too much.

'All right.'

They walked briskly on and began talking about the new English teacher. Had Moth noticed the bracelet round her ankle? Jane had seen her in the holidays, in the park, with a man with a moustache and untidy hair. Could he have been her husband? Or perhaps he was her lover? They stopped on the corner for a few minutes, elaborating this into a wild fantasy. Then, unable to ignore the cold, they parted.

As Moth began to run the first flakes of snow whirled down. They were white hopes, each with their own delicate, intricate pattern. But Moth could think of only two things: that she was friends with Ruth again, and that she was very hungry.

Author's Note

Although this is an imaginary story, the background is real and I would like to thank the following people for their help: Miss Eve Pettinger, who found time in her busy life as a teacher to tell me about *The Nutcracker* and who allowed me to watch her training the children for it; Mrs M. I. Jack, the principal of the Arts Educational Schools, who gave me permission to watch classes in London and at Tring; the London Festival Ballet, who let me attend a couple of rehearsals of *The Nutcracker*; Miss Hazel Vincent Wallace OBE, Managing Director of the Thorndike Theatre (Leatherhead) Limited, who let me attend a couple of rehearsals of their pantomime, *Sinbad the Sailor*; Mrs Betty Laine of the Laine Theatre Arts School, Epsom; Dick Condon, General Manager of the Theatre Royal, Norwich, who spared time to show me round the theatre; and Miss Elizabeth Roy, my editor, who made some very helpful suggestions.

If you have enjoyed this book you may like to read some more Knight titles:

SPOTLIGHT ON BALLET

IAN WOODWARD

Essential reading for dancers and ballet-goers alike. With a foreword by Royal Ballet star Wayne Eagling, this book looks at the history of ballet, its dancers, music, stories, steps, training, costume and the future directions of dance.

'Keep this book by you. Take it with you when you go to the ballet. Refer to it constantly. It is your passport to a wonderful theatrical experience – and besides, to a great deal of knowledge'. *Wayne Eagling*

KNIGHT BOOKS

THE FIRST STEP

JEAN RICHARDSON

The story of Moth Graham's first year at ballet school in London; her ups and downs, successes and failures, while adjusting to being away from home for the first time in her life. This book will strike an immediate chord with anyone who, like Moth, has longed to be able to dance.

THE SWISH OF THE CURTAIN

PAMELA BROWN

A revised edition of a much-loved theatre novel first published nearly forty years ago. It is the story of a group of children who set up their own repertory company – the Blue Door Theatre – and the problems that they have to overcome if they are to be taken seriously by their parents and friends and, most important of all, by the judge of the Seymore Trophy acting competition.

KNIGHT BOOKS

☐ 25547 1	SPOTLIGHT ON BALLET	95p
☐ 24030 X	THE FIRST STEP	75p
☐ 04145 5	THE SWISH OF THE CURTAIN	95p

All these books are available at your local bookshop or newsagent, or can be ordered direct from the publisher. Just tick the titles you want and fill in the form below.

Prices and availability subject to change without notice.

KNIGHT BOOKS, P.O. Box 11, Falmouth, Cornwall.

Please send cheque or postal order, and allow the following for postage and packing:

U.K. – 40p for one book, plus 18p for the second book, and 13p for each additional book ordered up to a £1.49 maximum.

B.F.P.O. and EIRE – 40p for the first book, plus 18p for the second book, and 13p per copy for the next 7 books, 7p per book thereafter.

OTHER OVERSEAS CUSTOMERS – 60p for the first book, plus 18p per copy for each additional book.

Name ....

Address ....

....